MW01595203

Miracles Beyond Medicine

Gloria Teague

PublishAmerica
Baltimore

First printing

For Dr. Jeter-
Thanks for holding me
together + for your kindness
Gloria

ISBN: 1-4137-1280-0
PUBLISHED BY PUBLISHAMERICA, LLLP
www.publishamerica.com
Baltimore

Printed in the United States of America

For my husband, Al.
You believed in me when I couldn't believe in myself.

Introduction

This book is about medical doctors, nurses and technicians that have personally witnessed miracles. These are stories about the bravery and faith of patients who were given a death sentence by doctors—these are people that only God could save.

We are now all believers. We've seen miracles beyond medicine.

CONTENTS

The Tie That Binds

Every critically ill patient that is admitted to the hospital leaves some type of lasting impression on the lives of the medical personnel they come in contact with. It's true that some, more than others, create an impact on our minds, on our hearts. Such was the case with Robert.

From Robert's words and his medical report, I pieced together what happened before he was transferred to my floor. As the nurse in charge, I was always careful to know all I could about each of my patients. I admit, to save my sanity, I try to *not* know more than is necessary about their personal life. My biggest concern is their physical problem.

It was a Friday evening and I was in the middle of a sixteen-hour shift. Hospitals all over the city were short-staffed and ours was no different. I'd just gotten a patient report phoned in from ER when I heard the rubber wheels on a transport gurney rolling down the hall. Knowing this was my new admit, I stood up to walk into the room across from the nursing station to greet my new patient.

He was a young man with dark hair and soulful brown eyes. The pallor of his skin blended in well with the crisp hospital sheets on his bed. Beside him walked a slim woman with long, flaming red hair. Not even the worry on her face could mar her beauty. They were holding hands in a white-knuckled grip. It was obvious these two were deeply in love, and terrified.

After the orderlies lifted him onto his bed from the gurney, I smiled my appreciation of their help. With a casual two-finger salute, they strolled from the room. I opened the chart they had left with me to scan over the front sheet.

"So, this is Robert? Hello, Dear. My name is Mary and I'll be your nurse tonight. I'll be here until 11 p.m., so we have plenty of time to get to know each other better."

Robert smiled weakly and turned to the redhead still clutching his hand. It was then that I noticed he was wearing a wedding band.

"Robert, is this your wife?"

His smile widened. "No, but we're engaged. This is Denyse, my future wife. We have a wedding date set for five weeks from tomorrow."

"Oh, I'm sorry. I just happened to notice the wedding ring on your finger and I thought…"

Unexpectedly, a large tear rolled down Denyse's lovely face. Robert brought her hand to his lips and kissed her palm.

"It's gonna be okay, baby."

Denyse began to shake her head in a vigorous denial. Then just as abruptly, her tears stopped, she wiped her eyes and smiled.

"Yes Robert, it *is* going to be okay."

Robert pulled his gaze from his fiancée long enough to flash a brilliant smile in my direction.

"Isn't she great? Isn't she beautiful? God, I love this woman so much."

I smiled again, then began the admission routine.

"Robert, what brought you to the ER?"

The grin slipped from his face and he turned his full attention to me.

"It's my back. It started hurting a couple of weeks ago. I thought I'd pulled something helping a friend move, but now I'm not so sure. Anyway, when I got up this morning, I could barely walk. The pain was so bad that I broke down and called Denyse to drive me here. It has to be bad for me to do that. I hate doctors and hospitals. Oh sorry— no offense."

I chuckled, "None taken. Do you have any other health problems that may have contributed to this, or any you feel I should know about?"

Denyse's head dropped and Robert stared at the ceiling, as if looking for an answer there. A frown formed between his eyebrows as he took a deep breath.

"Yeah, I have cancer."

I began flipping through the pages of the chart but was so surprised I couldn't seem to focus. Robert looked fairly healthy though he was quite thin. I suppose a terminal illness was the last thing I expected to hear him tell me.

The speaker box on the wall of the room squawked. "Mary, there's a Dr. Henning on the phone for you."

Grateful for the excuse to leave the room to regroup my thoughts, I apologized to both of them.

"I'm sorry. I'll be right back. Doctors get a bit testy when kept waiting. I'll go over your chart before I come back, Robert, so I'll be more familiar with your case."

His even white teeth gleamed, "Sure, take all the time you want. I don't think I'm going anywhere for a while. Besides, I have this gorgeous woman to keep me company."

I laughed, but it sounded forced even to my own ears.

When I finished with the doctor on the phone, I pulled Robert's medical chart toward me. It was easier to pull than lift it, so massive was its size. I began with the cover sheet that gave personal information on the patient.

Robert Wright: S/W/M, age 23

Occupation: computer technician

Chief complaint: severe back pain

Previous medical history: cancer of right hip and pelvic bone

Previous medical treatment: chemotherapy administered in TX

Prognosis: at the patient's request, chemotherapy was discontinued. Pt was told his life expectancy was two years or less

I opened the chart to the back sheets that contained earlier medical records. According to what I read, Robert's chemotherapy had been nearly two years ago.

I turned my head from side to side to loosen the knots caused by a tightening in my neck. I closed my eyes and massaged my temples, which had begun to throb more with each line I read in the young man's

11

chart. Several times my vision blurred as I ran my finger down the long list of tests that had been conducted, and the ones yet to be completed.

I lifted the phone and dialed the number for ER, to speak to a triage nurse. It was as I was again speaking to the nurse that had taken care of Robert that I began to cry.

"Hi Mary. What can I tell you that isn't in the chart? Only that Robert and his fiancée were told that he has only two options. One is he be admitted for chemotherapy, or two, go home to call Hospice to make him comfortable until he dies. Robert said he'd promised himself he'd never go through chemo again. He was advised that is his only chance. He asked how long he had, that he was getting married in five weeks. The doctor in attendance told him he wouldn't be able to get married then because he would, in all probability, be dead. There was a lot of crying. Robert then asked his fiancée to get out the wedding ring she had bought for him. He told her to put it on his finger. At first she resisted; she said it was for the wedding. After she thought about what the doctor said, she put the ring on his finger. The fiancée begged Robert to do the chemo, to give them a few more weeks. Robert being admitted shows that he intends to do so. This is a sad one, Mary. Right now I'm glad I'm in ER and not in your shoes."

I agreed. Right about now I envied her brief association with each patient. I knew that, in all likelihood, I was going to watch this young man die. It's never easy to lose a patient, but this one was going to be especially heart wrenching.

I squared my shoulders and walked back into Robert's room. Denyse was sitting beside him on the bed, both of them deep in what appeared to be a painful discussion. I imagined that any discussion between them at this point was going to be painful.

"Robert, I've been going over your chart and see that you've had chemo before."

A dark looked passed over his face.

"Yeah, I did. I hated it and said I'd die before I'd do it again. Well, it seems it's come down to that now. It's just that, all of a sudden, I've got a reason to live, so I guess we're gonna do the chemo thing again."

Denyse's look was one of love, and sadness. She spoke for the first time.

"Robert didn't want to do this, but I begged him to. I admit I know nothing about chemo, but I've heard it's pretty bad. I don't want to make him worse; I just want to keep him a little longer. He's got a wedding to go to, and he's not getting out of it that easily."

Her desperate attempt at humor did little to dispel the thick cloud of hopelessness that was almost palpable.

"Let's begin with you telling me, from the beginning, what brought you to the ER and go from there."

"The pain I've been having in my back just kept getting worse and worse. When I first got here, they thought it might be a kidney stone. God, right about now I wished they had been right. I guess the urine specimen and x-rays ruled that out. So next we went to a, uh... What was that test called Denyse?"

Softly, almost a whisper, "A CT scan."

"Yeah, that's it, a scan. I guess it was after the scan they decided the cancer has come back and is spreading to my spine."

Robert held his breath for a second, composing himself. Silent tears coursed down Denyse's cheeks.

"Well, anyway... They wound up telling me it's chemo or death. Which is silly, 'cause it's gonna be death anyway."

Denyse grasped his hand, "But we can have a few more weeks, Robert."

Tears swam in his eyes. "I'm not sure of that, honey, but I'm willing to give it a shot."

I cleared my throat and began to tell them what would happen next.

"Okay, here's the game plan. Evidently, they don't think you can glow in the dark yet so they're going to take more x-rays and another CT scan. We're going to take so much blood you'll swear we're supporting a vampire. It says in your chart that we may be doing an ultrasound, too. You know what that is, Robert?"

"Yeah, yeah, yeah, I know what that is. I'm sorry. I don't mean to sound cranky. I'm just tired and hurting."

"Well, that's one thing I can do something about, Robert. You've got orders for a pain injection every three hours if you want it. It will help the pain and you might even catch a few minutes sleep between tests. Want me to go get it now?"

He looked at Denyse and she nodded.

"Yes, Robert, take the shot. We can talk when you wake up completely, okay?"

I met the x-ray technician in Robert's room when I took the syringe of medication to him.

"Oh no, you don't. You just hold on one minute until I can give him this shot, then you can move him."

Robert had been gone to x-ray for about fifteen minutes when I heard muffled sobs coming from his room. Against my better judgment, I walked across the hall. Denyse was sitting in a chair, bent at the waist, her arms wrapped around a pillow with her face buried. When she saw me come in, she took a deep breath, wiped her eyes and stopped crying.

"I'm sorry. I thought no one would hear me. I don't mean to act so weak. In front of Robert I try so hard to be strong, to not break down. Sometimes I can do it, other times I can't."

Alarms sounding in my head, I sat down beside her and put my arms around her quivering shoulders.

"Want to talk about it? Would that help?"

"I don't know. What good will talking do? It's simple; Robert is going to die and there's nothing I can do about it. I'm hurt, I'm sad, but mostly I'm mad."

"I can understand…"

Her face was twisted into a grimace of anger.

"Do you? Unless you've lost the only man you've ever loved, you can't understand how I feel. Oh, I'm so sorry…"

"No, honey, it's okay. And you're right; I don't know how you feel. But I've been told I'm a great listener."

Denyse moved from beneath my arms and began to pace the room. The more she walked, the more she talked. I just sat quietly, letting her vent her feelings.

"I've been on the phone, calling everyone I know, asking them to pray for Robert. His name is now on more prayer lists than I even know about, I'm sure. A dear friend of ours, David, came by E.R. and prayed with Robert for a long time. David feels like this can be turned around if only we believe…"

The tone of her monologue turned from one of anguish to that of rage. I didn't blame her.

"This isn't fair! He's so kind, and he tries so hard to be a good person. Why can't it be someone else that's dying? Why not some scum of the earth, like a drunk or drug addict? Why can't God take a man that beats his wife, or mistreats his kids? Why Robert? He's only twenty-three years old! This is so wrong! I hate this!"

At this point she fell across Robert's bed and held her face in his pillow. All the anguish she was feeling soaked the pillow, yet it muffled the screams of anger she was experiencing.

I sat beside her and stroked her long, silky hair. I crooned to her as I would one of my own children, not making promises, just making comforting noises. There was nothing else I could do. I couldn't give Robert a longer life. I couldn't make him live long enough to repeat his wedding vows. I couldn't help him to grow old with the woman he loved.

We both heard Robert's voice at the same moment. He was joking with the transport person as they made their way down the long hall. Denyse jumped up and ran to the bathroom. I heard water running and knew she was trying to wash away any evidence of her tears. But Robert would know, and he would love her more because of it.

When I went in to pick up Robert's dinner tray later that evening, I saw he hadn't touched it. He and Denyse were staring at the flickering images on the wall-mounted TV set as if they were actually watching it. They both smiled at me when I walked in the room.

"Robert, how are you feeling, dear? Need anything for pain? It's been quite a while now since you've had a shot. It's late and it could help you sleep."

"I'm not really in that much pain, to tell you the truth. Tell you what I would like to have, though. Can you get a blanket for Denyse? She's freezing."

He smiled at her and she grinned.

"Robert, I'm not the one that's in the hospital, honey. I'm fine. Take your shot and go to sleep."

"Nope, not until you get a blanket and I can see you're dozing off. Then I'll get the shot."

Denyse shook her head in mock consternation.

"Stubborn men! Okay, if that's what it takes, you got a deal."

I handed her a blanket from the closet and she curled up in the chair next to Robert's bed.

"Well, ready for that shot now, Robert?"

"Yeah, I guess so."

As I was administering the injection, Robert talked to me.

"You know, I've never seen so many doctors in one room like they were in E.R. I had seven of them in there with me. Talk about crowded! Oh well, seven's a lucky number, isn't it, Mary?"

"It sure is, Robert. Try to get some sleep now. You're going to have a full day tomorrow."

He groaned, "Yeah, I know."

He then turned on his side, facing Denyse and watched her fall asleep.

I checked on both of them many times throughout the night. Each time, they were both sound asleep.

When I clocked out at 7 a.m., I was weary in body and heart.

It seemed as if I'd only just left when I walked back into Robert's room that afternoon. I noticed that Denyse had either left long enough to change clothes, or someone had brought her something else to wear. Both of them greeted me with their now-familiar smiles.

"Hi there, Mary, Mary, quite contrary."

Denyse giggled. "Oh Robert, that was so corny."

"Yeah well, corny is as corny does."

She groaned. "Oh yeah, that's so much better, honey."

"How are you feeling this morning, Robert?"

"I'm feeling pretty good. My back still hurts, but nothing like it did when I first came in here."

"Well, that's good. Feel like eating this afternoon?"

"Yeah, I do. I'm really hungry."

I was carrying his lunch tray in to him when Robert's physicians blocked my path. I put the tray back on the serving cart then went in to stand by my patient as he was given the bad news.

Just as Robert had said, there were seven of them. The small room had suddenly gotten crowded.

Dr. Fields was evidently going to be the spokesman for the group. "Good morning, Robert. Denyse, I doubt you slept very well in that chair last night."

The young couple replied in cautious tones of voices. Both of them wore a look of dread on their faces.

"Come on, kids. It's okay to smile, you know. I understand—we haven't given you one single reason to smile. Yesterday we pretty much blew your world apart. Well, I believe you're going to like us much better today."

The look of dread was replaced by one of suspicion. I, myself, felt as if I was holding my breath, afraid to hear the doctor's next words.

Robert's voice was shaky, "Okay, I'll bite. What are you talking about?"

Dr. Fields chuckled, "Not going to allow yourself any false hopes, right? Good, that's a smart thing to do. We want to talk to you about your test results." Some of the other doctors began to nod their heads. I saw Robert swallow hard and Denyse's eyes opened wider. Dr. Fields continued.

"When you first came in here, Robert, it didn't look good. From all indications, it appeared that not only had the cancer come back, but also it had spread to your spine. We suggested chemotherapy to try to combat the assault, but to be truthful, we didn't hold out much hope that it would work. The most we could have hoped for was to buy you a few more days, or being optimistic, a few more weeks."

Robert's eyes were now as large as Denyse's.

"You're speaking in past tense."

Dr. Fields smile covered his entire face.

"Yep, I sure am. Robert, this is going to be hard for you to believe. Denyse, hold onto your seat. The tests we ran yesterday are completely different from the ones we ran when you were in E.R. In fact, they don't even look like they were done on the same person. The difference is astounding."

The young couple took each other's hands, allowing hope a small opening. Dr. Fields stepped closer to the bed, his smile growing more with each sentence.

"Robert, the cancer is gone."

Even I gasped. Denyse stood as if shot from her chair. Robert sat up straighter in the bed. He was so surprised he could barely get his question out.

"Just what does this mean? What exactly are we talking about here?"

"Okay, let me attempt to explain this. Attempt is all I can do, believe me. Test results from yesterday showed no reoccurrence of cancer. Not only has it not spread, we can't find any evidence of a tumor. We are able to see the thinning of the bone around your right hip and pelvic region, which is normal after chemotherapy. From what all of us have seen, the biggest problem you'll have is that these areas will ache more, possibly have more arthritis than the rest of your body, when you get older."

Denyse held up her hand to stop him.

"Wait… What did you just say?"

Dr. Fields seemed to almost glow with happiness, himself.

"That's right, Denyse. I said 'when you get older.' Robert, looks like if you want to get out of this wedding, you're going to have to find another excuse."

Robert, still fearful to accept what he was hearing, wanted to understand.

"But, how did it happen? Did the tests get mixed up? Are you sure you're talking about my body? There's no confusion? I don't get it."

"Neither do we, Robert, but let's discuss this. Now, if you're a pragmatic person, you might think that there was some type of spontaneous remission, and be totally confused by how it all came about. Out of the seven of us, that's the professional opinion of four. Then there are three of us that have a different theory altogether. We three are Christians, and firmly believe the hand of God altered your physical body. I believe, with all my heart Robert, that we're looking at a miracle. So, if you want to be logical, you can rub your chin and say 'Hmm.' If you believe in God, get down on your knees and thank Him because he just gave you back your life."

Denyse threw her arms around Robert, joyful tears coursing down her face, and laughed.

"Robert! Oh, Robert! We're going to get married!"

Dr. Fields took one of Robert's hands and shook it.

"Robert, you better marry this girl in a hurry. I believe she loves you."

Both Robert and Denyse were laughing and crying so hard that they didn't notice when the doctors left the room. I closed the door behind me to give them privacy and time to grasp what they'd just been told.

An hour later I handed Robert his discharge orders.

"You're to follow up with your family doctor, Robert. I have a prescription for muscle relaxers and mild pain medication. According to the doctor, your official diagnosis is now a pulled muscle." I couldn't stop smiling.

Robert hugged Denyse so hard I was sure he'd break her ribs.

"Let's go home, honey. We got a wedding to plan!"

I insisted on being the one that took Robert downstairs in a wheelchair. After he was sitting in the car, Denyse came to me and gave me a hug.

"Mary, we want you to come to our wedding, if you can. It's not going to be a big affair; just people that mean the most to us will be there. We would be honored if you would come."

Tears clouded my vision.

"Well, send me an invitation and I just might."

I watched as they drove away from the hospital and they waved until they were out of sight.

Five weeks from that day, I attended a wedding. Denyse was beautiful in her dress with the long train trailing behind her as she walked down the aisle. Robert was handsome in his black tuxedo, wearing the biggest smile I've ever seen as his bride walked toward him.

The words of the wedding vows had never seemed so poignant before.

With tears of happiness, they both joyfully repeated, "…In sickness and in health, till death do us part…"

A Grandmother's Love

The house was burning, smoke spiraled skyward; flames licking the cold late winter day, and the sleet rushing to the ground did little more than keep the fire from completely engulfing the tired old house. In one of the bedrooms, a young woman lay in a puddle of blood that surrounded her still body. Her breathing had stopped several minutes before the fire was started in an attempt to cover up her murder. She had been viciously, fatally, beaten and then stabbed. She died never knowing the horrors that were to be committed against her niece, the little girl she had loved more than life itself.

The child lay beneath a dilapidated bed in an empty trailer down the street. She was shivering, bleeding, and blessedly unconscious after the man had tried to kill her. She was hemorrhaging from the wound made by a butter knife being shoved into her neck, just after she'd been slammed, repeatedly, against her aunt's bedroom walls, so hard that part of her brain died. Deep furrowed marks illustrated how she had been forcefully pushed across the rotten wood of the sagging floor, and roaches scuttled across and around her body. Her auburn hair fanned out around her pale face. She made no sound, not even a whimper that would alert passerby to her presence. Her name was Amy, and she was only four years old.

The day had started out as each one that preceded it. Mary would wake up early, around five AM, and begin getting ready for her shift at the restaurant where she worked as a waitress. She would cook breakfast at six o'clock, and Amy would pad into the kitchen about fifteen minutes later, being awakened by the smell of the delicious food her aunt always prepared for her and Sean, her boyfriend.

Amy smiled as she ate, and Mary had a difficult time finishing her work preparations because she kept going over to Amy to kiss and tickle her. Amy would giggle and playfully push her hands away, all the time chortling, "More, more! Tickle me, Mommy!" She would raise one of his arms and say, "Tickle Amy right here, Mommy", then try to cover it with her other hand so Mary would have to work harder to tickle her. All the while, she would giggle almost nonstop. It was a game they had played ever since Mary had taken Amy to raise after her own sister had been killed in a car accident. Amy had only been one year old when she lost her mother. To Mary, Amy was her child. To Amy, this was her mother, never remembering the woman that had given birth to her.

At 6:45, Mary went in to wake Sean so he could take care of Amy and eat his own breakfast. Since he was out of work, they saved money on a babysitter for her niece. But things were getting tight, financially, and Sean was going to have to get a job soon. They were sinking in a river of debt. The more they floundered, the worse Sean's temperament became. He was getting surly, and more short-tempered with each week that passed. In fact, Mary was afraid she was going to have to ask him to move out. She didn't want Amy exposed to Sean's angry outbursts anymore. It was happening too frequently, and her first priority was keeping her baby healthy and happy.

This morning, as most mornings lately, Sean awoke in a bad mood. Mary saw it on his face the moment he opened his eyes. He didn't speak to her, merely glared at her kiss to wake him. The look caused her to step back from the bed and sigh.

"Sean, breakfast is ready. Amy is already eating and yours is getting cold. I have to hurry or I'll be late for work. I sure hope that old car starts and the roads aren't too icy this morning. I put a load of laundry in the washer. Would you please throw that in the dryer later? I have to run! Bye honey. You and Amy have fun today."

Sean's only response was to sit up on the side of the bed and swing his long, muscular legs to the floor. He propped his elbows on his knees

22

and dropped his head into his hands. He held up one hand to stop Mary from kissing him goodbye.

Mary rushed into the kitchen, kissed a grinning Amy one more time, told her to be a good girl and eat all her breakfast, then she ran for the car, sliding on the slick sidewalk in front of the house.

As the engine was idling, she stared at the home she shared with her child and Sean. It needed a coat of paint, badly, and she was trying to save enough money to buy new drapes. All those worries were undermined by her concern about Sean's depression, or whatever it was that had him so angry. She sighed again as she pulled away from the hurtful silence of her home.

Sean shuffled into the kitchen, poured a cup of coffee and lit a cigarette. He only glanced at Amy as he opened the newspaper to the classified ads, in search of the elusive job that would raise him from the pit of poverty. He found an ad that looked interesting and set his cup of coffee down. When he folded the page of the paper, he brushed against the cup setting too close to the edge of the table, spilling the hot liquid onto Amy's bare legs.

Amy reacted instantly by screaming loudly. She jumped from her chair, knocking her plate to the floor. Wet scrambled eggs and buttered toast slid across the floor, adding to the mess of the coffee already there.

"Shut up, stupid! God, all the hell you ever do is cry! I'm so sick of hearing you bawling. You're a spoiled little brat, and your aunt's a bitch that babies you to death."

Instead of soothing the little girl, his loud angry words frightened the child even more than the pain of the burn on both legs. She cried harder, louder, staring at Sean with wide eyes filled with tears. Her innocent, sweet face didn't soften the anger bubbling up inside Sean.

Sean jerked Amy up by one arm, dragging her into the bedroom. He threw the child on the bed, then turned to find clean clothes to put on her. His violent actions scared Amy even more and she began to sob from fright.

"I'm not going to tell you again, girl! Shut that up or I'll give you something to *really* cry about! You hear me, you brat?"

Amy buried her wet face in the pillow where her mother lay her head, and cried in huge gulping sobs. Sean's explosive shouts of rage did nothing more than make her more frantic.

Sean leaned over the bed and slapped Amy's bottom, the sound echoing around the room. The sting of the blow wasn't as harsh as the fear that Amy felt. She began to scream.

Sean picked the girl up, slapping her face, over and over. As he hit the little face, he would scream at the child to shut up. Amy was unable to do so.

The screaming grew louder till Sean thought he would lose his mind if it didn't stop. He doubled up his fist and hammered the little girl in the face, breaking her nose.

Momentarily, pain caused Amy to stop crying. It was difficult to cry when the shocked pain overshadowed everything else in the world. Then the numbness began to rapidly fade, and Amy began to scream, even louder than before.

Sean threw the little girl back onto the mattress, where she landed on her stomach. While her face was shoved into the quilt her grandmother had made, Sean pummeled Amy's back with huge, cruel fists. Her breath knocked from her lungs, Amy gasped for breath. Sean then picked up the girl and threw her across the room with all his strength.

When Amy's broken body fell to the floor next to the shattered portrait of herself and Mary, Sean picked her up, and slammed the small child against the wall, again and again, until Amy could no longer cry or even moan.

Throughout the day, Sean watched television, turning his attention from the flickering images on the screen only when Amy would move or groan. He would heave a heavy sigh as if this was a distasteful job he must endure, then pick the girl up from the littered floor to once again throw her against the wall that was now blood-splattered.

At 3:30, Mary arrived home. The first thing she noticed was the breakfast dishes still on the kitchen table, food all over the floor and the wet clothes still in the washer.

"Sean? What happened in here? Why is there such a mess? Why

didn't you at least do the dishes? And I had hoped you would empty the washer."

There was no reply and the house was quiet as a tomb.

"Sean?" Concern now lined her face.

"Amy?"

With a deep sense of foreboding, Mary walked into the bedroom where she heard the tinny sounds of the TV.

Her eyes widened when she saw the room was in total disarray. She saw Sean sitting on the side of the bed, much in the same position he had been in when she had left for work. She then saw the dented sheetrock splattered with blood.

"Amy? Sean! Where's my baby?"

When she saw her tiny body lying motionless on the floor, Mary screamed.

She ran across the room and knelt in the broken glass to touch her child's shattered face. A sorrowful moan passed her lips when she saw the injuries that had been inflicted on her baby. With a mother's rage, she turned on the one person she knew had done this.

"You bastard! You did this! You hurt my baby! I'll kill you!"

She jumped on the bed, not taking time to walk around it, and began to claw at Sean's back with her fingernails. She punched him, bit his ears, and kicked him as hard as her slender legs would allow. As she was venting terrorized anger at her baby's condition, Sean was hitting her with his fists, but she was too angry to notice.

It was only when Sean grabbed a butter knife he had been using to adjust the television set and stabbed her in the face, did she stop fighting him. But even though she was still, he stabbed her over two dozen times, not stopping until his arm grew tired from the force of the blows.

As if she felt her mother's death, Amy moaned and moved, trying to rise from the floor. Sean strolled across the bloody room and nonchalantly kicked the already broken ribs. When Amy opened her mouth to scream, Sean shoved the gore-speckled knife into the girl's throat. Amy stopped moving.

Disgusted with the very sight of the little girl, Sean folded the ragged carpet remnant that Amy lay on over the still little body. He lifted her into his arms and walked out the back door of the house.

Unmindful of the bitter cold, Sean casually walked across the brown grass to the crumbling trailer down the street that had been abandoned for over a year. The rusty door hung open, and this is where he threw the body he carried. He was so tired from physical exertion, he didn't get the carpet-laden bundle far enough into the filthy opening so he knelt on the crumbling floor, and shoved Amy further into the darkness.

Sean then strolled back into the hellacious scene he had created. As he stood staring at Mary's dead body, he was thinking of a way to avoid being charged with double homicide.

He opened the back door and picked up a can partially filled with gasoline he used for the lawnmower. He took it into the bedroom and drizzled the liquid over Mary's body and as much of the bedroom furniture as he could before the gas was depleted. He grabbed a few things from the dresser, stood at the open door of the room, lit a match, and threw it in.

Sean stood for a few seconds, watching the blue flames eat at the mattress, the faded drapes, then finally Mary's clothing. Secure in the belief that it would be ruled an accident, Sean walked out the front door while the smoke alarm shrilled in the kitchen.

He was glad to see no smoke coming from the house as he pulled from the driveway. He drove down the street at a sedate rate of speed, not wanting to alert the neighbors too soon by his haste.

It would be another five minutes before a call went in to the 911 operator, reporting a fire. No, the caller didn't know if anyone was home. The car wasn't in the driveway, so hopefully, the nice young woman and her baby that lived there were gone somewhere.

The sirens and the flashing strobe lights of the fire trucks and police cars shocked the normally quiet neighborhood. The street quickly filled with both the curious and the concerned. All were eager to tell the officers of the people who lived in the burning house. They talked about the sweet young waitress and her beautiful daughter, Amy. They were just as quick to criticize the angry young man, Sean, that had moved in with the mother and daughter a few months before.

Firefighters rushed into the flames, anxious to ascertain that the building was, indeed, empty. It didn't take them long, even with the fire and smoke, to find the body of Mary lying on the floor of the partially burned bedroom.

The fire was quickly under control and paramedics ran in to assess the patient. They knew immediately that she was dead. They spoke in hushed tones with the fire Marshall standing outside. They told him they had seen the body, and they were certain the lady had not died from the fire. To them, it appeared she had been stabbed before the fire was started.

Officers then began to question the people gathered in the front yard of the destroyed home. One thing they kept hearing was inquiries as to the whereabouts of the baby. They all asked, "But where's Amy?"

Two of the neighbors related that they had heard yelling and cursing earlier in the day. It seemed like a heated argument was going on just before the fire broke out. Everyone was generous with his or her scornful description of Sean. The police issued an all-points bulletin on the man they assumed had kidnapped the baby and fled after he had killed Mary.

The smoldering body was removed from the house, and neighbors cried when they saw the body bag being put into the ambulance. Fear for little Amy's life was uppermost in everyone's heart.

An hour after Mary was taken to the morgue, Sean was picked up by police in a small town fifty miles away. His car had run out of gas, and he was hitchhiking to the nearest bus station. It had been his intention to leave the state as quickly as possible.

The car was searched meticulously, but no sign was found of Amy. After he was arrested, it took the police another forty-five minutes of grueling questioning to get him to admit he had never taken the girl, that he had left the child near her mother. At no time did Sean tell them what he had done, nor did he tell them the location of Amy.

The police went back to the house where Amy had lived. They searched every room, in every closet, beneath every bed, behind every item of furniture. The only sign they discovered of the little girl was her blood covering the only bedroom wall untouched by the fire. People came into the yard to volunteer their services and spread throughout the neighborhood, even going door to door, asking if anyone had seen Amy.

It was as dawn began to fully settle onto the hushed street that a female officer stumbled across Amy. She found her by pure luck, not by any sound she had heard or any other clues to help her. The abandoned trailer had been searched many times, but no one had looked *under* the wood, bugs, and garbage that littered the floor. It was there that she found the baby.

Amazingly, Amy was still alive, though broken, bleeding, and near death from the freezing temperatures alone. The officer opened her thick jacket, unbuttoned her shirt, and then wrapped Amy inside, next to her warmth, next to her heart.

She clasped the child to her as she ran to the ambulance that had been summoned. The paramedics tried to take Amy from her, but she pushed them aside, climbed into the back of the ambulance, and yelled for them to hurry. She told them the baby was barely alive and they had to get her to the hospital immediately.

I was on duty when little Amy was brought into the emergency room. The sight of any child sick or injured affects us, but what had been done to this small body shocked and angered everyone in attendance.

A pediatric specialist was called in to assist in saving Amy's life. At this point, none of us thought there was much hope of that, but we had to try. Every test that was ordered was issued a STAT, for we knew we were battling the enemy time.

Amy was put on a ventilator to help her breathe. Since her throat had been destroyed by the blunt knife, the plastic tube that helped pump oxygen into her lungs had to be put in her broken nose. We covered her body with warming blankets, trying to raise her body temperature. Once she was being ventilated, we were allowed to do a further assessment of her injuries.

All the ribs on one side of her small body were broken. Her kidneys were bruised and her spleen was ruptured. CAT scans showed an alarming amount of swelling to the brain which required immediate surgery to relieve the pressure.

Both of her green eyes were filled with blood, as were her ears. One arm was broken, and her entire body was covered with angry bruises and bloody cuts.

The attending physician called for surgery to get an O.R. STAT, and we ran down the hall with our tiny patient, praying it wasn't too late.

Amy was in surgery for many hours. At times, the surgeon was sure she wasn't going to live through the tedious operation. Amy's family was called in to let them know she was alive, barely, and fighting for her very life.

As we waited for word of the baby's condition, we heard how Sean had relayed the events of the day to the police, after they questioned him into exhaustion. Mary's mother, Helen, cried as she told us the terrible things he had done to her baby girl, and the things he'd done to Amy. We were silent, not daring to voice what we were feeling. Helen was heartbroken and upset, but she was yet to see the tiny body we were working on. We knew, had she been in our shoes, and had seen what we had seen, her heartbreak would turn into an anger few people ever know. It is an anger fueled by hatred, from wanting to hurt, maim, even kill, the person that had perpetrated this horrendous crime against an innocent child.

We comforted the family as much as was humanly possible and waited out the hours Amy was in surgery. Every minute that went by, we were sure the doctor would come out of O.R. with the sad news that the baby had died of her massive injuries.

Helen, alone, had enough faith to move mountains. She talked about taking care of Amy when she got well, of having her play in her front yard, and helping her plant the flowers she loved to pick in the spring. I'm ashamed to say that none of the staff shared her belief.

Amy survived surgery, but the prognosis wasn't good. There was massive damage done to the right side of her brain and it was believed she was deaf, blind, paralyzed, and mute. The surgeons were quick to point out that none of this was conclusive and only after Amy had healed would we know the true extent of long term damage.

Helen was taken to Amy's bed in the pediatric intensive care unit. When she saw the machines, bandages, and the tiny body filled with tubes, she began to cry, softly. Even in the midst of her grief, she didn't want to alarm the little girl. She stroked her arm and picked up her small hand to curl her fist around her own trembling finger. She rubbed her leg and stroked her hair as she told her how much she loved her and would always take care of her. She talked to her about playing in the sunshine, and playing dress-up in grandma's old clothes.

The staff worked silently, eyes averted from the stark, mournful despair in Helen's face. We knew this was a private moment, and she needed it to begin the healing process. She had lost her only remaining child to a mad man, and she openly prayed that she be allowed to keep her granddaughter with her.

That evening, the local newscast carried the story, along with pictures of Amy, her aunt, and Sean. The community was outraged and cried out for no leniency for the monster that had committed the crimes against the young woman and the little girl.

Amy had a rough night, her breathing slowing to the point of near death several times. Each time, we thought it would be the end of the brave little girl.

As the morning light was cascading into the room that was filled with machines, an examination showed Amy's pupils were unequal and unresponsive. A STAT x-ray was ordered and it was discovered the swelling had resumed in her brain. O.R. was again readied to take the child into surgery.

Because of the local and national concern generated for Amy, impromptu news cast was given. While emergency room doctors and nurses spoke into the camera, Amy was having a shunt inserted inside her head to relieve the pressure of fluid building up there. Once again, she made it through surgery, and we were no less than amazed.

Amy was still sedated when she arrived back in PICU, but began to awaken shortly afterward as the nurse was changing her diaper. From the moment she opened her eyes, stare unfocused, the child started crying. She continued to cry almost continually for the next week. The specialist felt it was due to neurological damage and wasn't sure if it would ever end without the benefit of constant medication.

We also found that Amy wasn't able to follow simple commands, her eyes did not follow moving objects, and she didn't react to loud noise. When tests were conducted on her feet and legs, it was found she also didn't react to pain stimuli in those areas of the body. In short, Amy's diagnosis was severe brain damage, compounded by blindness, deafness, and paralysis. The outlook was quite grim for the child.

The news wasn't good for Helen, either. She had stayed with Amy around the clock since she had been brought to the hospital. Finally, exhausted to the point of tears, she admitted she needed help. Yet when she called family members to take her place at Amy's side so she could go home, sleep, take a shower, and get more clothes, no one would come. Each person she called had an excuse for being unable to stay with the child. It was as if they had turned their backs on Amy and Helen.

Helen summed it all up for us, "I'm not mad at them. I guess, in a way, I even understand. Unlike me, they've listened to what the doctors have to say about this baby, when they tell us there's little or no hope of Amy being normal, if she even lives. I guess I'm just too old and stubborn to accept that. I lost almost everything I had the day my child was murdered. I just can't give up on the love of her life, Amy, now. She would count on me to be here for her, and I love her too much to do anything else."

Helen then sank into a chair near Amy's bed and dissolved into harsh, racking sobs that tore at our hearts. We touched her arm, or gently stroked her hand, but we felt so helpless. What could we do, other than try to save her granddaughter's life? We weren't in the position to force other family members to help a tired grandma, or to love this little girl that needed all of them so much. It was at this moment that Amy awoke and began to cry once more. I was afraid for Helen's emotional well being, as her face was wet with sorrowful tears of near defeat.

Amy was sedated to allow her to rest and Helen fell into a fitful nap in the stiff, unyielding chair. I pulled the sheet up to the child's chin and draped a blanket over her loving grandmother, then prayed they both could get some rest.

Two hours later, alarms began to shrill throughout the unit. Helen awakened instantly and jumped to the side of Amy's bed. The machine was screaming out a warning that the pressure in her small, tired brain had yet again increased. The specialist was summoned, and he called the surgery department from the cell phone in his car.

Another stressful surgery commenced. As with each one before, we prayed, yet expected the worst. Helen proved she was made of sterner stuff, or had a deeper faith. She leaned her head on the side of Amy's bed and prayed.

Amy was placed in Helen's arms after she left recovery. So much had been done to her tiny body; we felt letting her hold her instead of placing Amy in her bed could do no further damage. She crooned to her and sang little girl songs, filled with the love and wonder of a kinder, gentler world. Perhaps it was her deep, abiding love, or the promise of God's saving grace that worked magic that night.

Amy opened her eyes and smiled at her grandma. She reached up to touch her nose and grinned when Helen's eyes opened wide in joy. She touched her grandmother's lips when her face was wreathed in a smile, then her hand slipped down to her arm, attempting to tickle her as her mother had always done to her. The room was filled with hushed awe and all our faces were wet with tears of happiness.

The last surgery proved to be successful. The swelling in the brain failed to reappear. When Amy touched Helen's face and grinned, we knew she wasn't blind, and some of her long-term memory was apparent, evidenced by her attempt to tickle her grandmother.

As news spread across the nation, toys, clothing, and gifts of all kinds were brought or sent to the hospital. Money to help defray medical expenses also poured in, and Helen never failed to thank God with each delivery.

Further testing, though, revealed that the prognosis for Amy was not as good as Helen hoped. Amy was blind in one eye, had permanent hearing loss, and a substantial amount of irreversible brain damage. In spite of this crushing announcement, Helen was happy. Amy was still alive, and the damage wasn't as bad as we first feared it would be. She told everyone that would listen that she truly believed Amy would be walking and talking by the end of the year. She seemed ready and willing to accept the responsibility of caring for her young charge.

Sean was charged with murder and is still in jail, awaiting trial.

One of the gifts Amy was given was a custom-built stroller donated by a national medical supply company which cost over $2,500.00. Last week, Amy was strapped into that stroller, and while wearing a pretty white hat and a bib that read "Special—and God loves me", she attended a news conference in one of the meeting rooms of the hospital.

The reason for all the celebration was the fact that Amy was going home with her grandmother who had never given up hope. Even though she faces extensive physical therapy and may never be the little girl she was meant to be before that cold winter day she was nearly killed, Amy had escaped the death certificate we thought would accompany her from the building.

I stood outside the room where the news conference was being conducted. I watched Helen answer the media's questions with a graciousness that I'll never forget. She wore a beatific smile that lit up the room as she said she believed in miracles, and that Amy was already proof of that.

"I want to thank the doctors, nurses, and technicians that took care of my Amy. But I want to offer praise to God, who in all His loving mercy, saved this child when all else failed. Lord, please take care of my little girl, and thank You for allowing me to keep my sweet little Amy."

As the Christmas season approaches, Amy has continued to amaze and delight rehabilitation workers at the hospital she was sent to in New Jersey. As promised by her grandmother, Amy is now walking and talking with all the excitement shown by any normal five-year-old. Her favorite pastime is dressing up in Mary's old clothes and smearing makeup all over her sweet little face. Next fall, she will attend kindergarten, a monumental accomplishment.

Unfailing Faith

Kim Sanders grinned through the noise of holiday chatter filling the van. She was driving home after Christmas shopping with her mother, mother-in-law, and her four-year-old son, Jamie. She reached down to pat her rounded stomach, silently loving the newest arrival to the family, due in three months. She heard whispers coming from the back seat; sure they were about gifts for her and Jamie. Secrets over, they began to talk in a normal tone, lovingly teasing each other as only families can do. The lively banter and excited plans reaching her ears made her smile. It would be the last time Kim would smile for a very long time.

It had been raining all day, a typical winter afternoon in the south. It was just cold enough to have a bite in the air. Kim was thankful the roads weren't icy. She began planning dinner, taking stock in her mind of the contents of the cabinets and freezer. She knew that Ron, her husband, would be famished after his shift. As the lead man in a foundry, he worked himself as hard as he worked his men. Supper would be fast and simple since she was worn out from all the walking they had done that day.

Jamie, buckled into the front passenger seat, leaned over to lay his blonde head on his mother's lap. His eyelids were fluttering and he valiantly fought to stay awake, sure he was going to hear that magical word mentioned one more time that day. "Santa" had been on Jamie's mind for weeks, and he grew more excited with each day that passed. He looked up into his mother's eyes, flashed that sweet, crooked grin that Kim loved so much, and fell asleep.

In the back seat, the two older women kept talking, though they lowered their voices when they noticed the youngest occupant of the van had finally given into the sleepiness that had threatened all afternoon.

Sara, Kim's mother, leaned toward her daughter, "Sweetheart, do you think we should have two or three pumpkin pies this year?"

Before she could offer a suggestion, Kim heard her mother-in-law, Jean, answer the question.

"Why don't we just have two and I'll bake a chocolate cake for dinner. Surely two pumpkin pies are enough. I know how much the men like the pie, but they need to accept change. I think we've spoiled all our men and it's time to bring them into the nineties."

The laughter bubbling up inside Kim stopped as she saw a black car careening toward them. The other driver had obviously lost control and had slid across the grassy median divider, straight at them. The car was rocking from the speed and had turned sideways when it reached the pavement on the other side of the four-lane highway.

Kim tensed and gripped the wheel of the van. She twisted the wheel to the left, and then back to the right, vainly trying to avoid the collision. It seemed that no matter which direction she chose, an accident was inevitable.

Beneath her heart, Jamie awoke just long enough to ask in a drowsy voice, "Mommy?"

The out-of-control vehicle flipped over once before it slammed into the front of the van. The force of the impact knocked the van backward into oncoming traffic, crashing into two other cars before it, too, began to roll, end over end. None of the passengers in those two cars were injured.

To Kim, it all seemed to happen in slow motion. She heard Sara and Jean scream. She heard Jamie's sharply inhaled breath of fear. Then, blessedly, she heard nothing else.

Kim awoke only once, and tried to turn her head to analyze the situation. She briefly felt mind-numbing pain throughout her body, but she didn't realize what had happened. She didn't know where she was, or how she gotten there. She had forgotten the accident, and the other people who had been involved. The quickly approaching twilight was filled with the flashing strobe lights of emergency vehicles. Traffic was blocked for miles. Urgent demands echoed in the cold night air, yelling for assistance, or yet another extraction tool to free the injured people in the van and car.

I was a staff nurse working in Surgical Intensive Care the night Kim was brought to our hospital. Because most of the unit had been empty, I was told to go to ER to meet the ambulance and to assist with the care of my next patient.

Kim was brought in on a machine we called "Thumper", an oxygen-powered machine that automatically compresses the chest as in CPR. I hated the sound of that machine, as it had always signified death in my mind. The "ka-THUNK, ka-THUNK" sound sent shivers down my spine.

The EMSA paramedics had already intubated Kim and were using the ambu bag to force oxygen into her lungs, one of which had already collapsed. The medics had also placed four by four gauze pads on various parts of Kim's body, securing them with rolls of tape. It seemed as if even they had given up trying to cover the massive injuries we found when Kim arrived.

Kim's head was the worst. Her lovely blonde hair was matted with blood, and I was shocked she was still alive when I saw the damage that had been done.

Most of her face was crushed, making it difficult to imagine what this young woman had looked like mere hours earlier. Her hands were also crushed, and the bones of her arms and legs were protruding in various locations. The evident trauma to this young woman paled by comparison, though, when we noticed her rounded stomach.

The trauma room became a battle zone. Doctors and nurses came from every corner of the emergency room, all eager to save this young woman. Doctor's orders were filled before they even had time to issue them, the nurses working as if one person. What may have appeared to be mass confusion was actually a smoothly-run Code Blue situation, a term given to announce loss of heartbeat and/or respiration.

As we worked, we moved fluidly with each other, yet were able to hear the paramedic's report.

"This is Kim Sanders. Twenty-five-year-old female. Driver of a van involved in a collision with a drunk driver. She's about six months pregnant. We detected no fetal heartbeat during transport. Her vitals are: no pulse, no spontaneous respiration. Intubated at the scene to establish an airway and to ventilate the patient."

The attending physician's lab coat was covered in blood. He took time to wipe his sweaty brow with the sleeve, then spoke to the paramedic as he continued to work.

"Was she the only person in the van?"

The paramedic hesitated before he answered, which caused all of us to quickly glance at him, urging him, with our silence, to answer the doctor.

"Uh, no. Mrs. Sanders was the driver, but there were three other people in the van."

The doctor's voice grew sharper, seeming to get irritated that he was having to force information from the medic.

"And? What happened to the other people, and who were they?"

"Mrs. Sanders' mother and mother-in-law were in the back seat. They are in serious condition at another hospital. Her four-year-old son was in the front with his mother."

Here, the paramedic stopped talking again. Once more, we nervously looked in his direction, but continued to work on Kim.

"Jamie, the little boy, died at the scene. He's the DOA you have in the next room."

Behind my clear, plastic safety goggles, my eyes filled with scalding unshed tears. I had never seen the child, but I mourned the loss of the little boy.

The doctor's voice was husky as he asked, "What about the driver of the car that hit them?"

Anger laced the hard-bitten answer from the paramedic; "The bastard's dead."

Though we are health-care workers, nurturers, we didn't chastise him for his feelings. As horrid as it sounds, we too, felt the same way. We were as angry, as disgusted, as the harried medic that stood at the foot of the cot that held Kim's destroyed body.

We placed a fetal heart monitor on Kim's distended stomach, hoping to get a heart rhythm, letting us know the baby was still alive. The monitor showed a perfectly flat-line.

Since it had been almost an hour since the accident and we didn't know how long the baby had been without a heartbeat, if there was any chance to save this baby's life, it was now or never. The doctor took one look at the monitor and yelled, "Call OR, STAT. Tell them they need all the help they can get."

One of the nurses and the respiratory care practitioner held onto the cot, the IV poles, and while still squeezing the ambu bag, raced down the hall toward the elevator, rushing Kim into surgery. I said a silent prayer as I made my way back to Surgical Intensive Care, hoping I would be using the ventilator I would set-up, preparatory to Kim's arrival after surgery.

While waiting to get word from surgery, I admitted a couple of other patients; both were emergency heart surgeries. They seemed stable, and would sleep the rest of the night comfortably.

Just before 5 AM, surgery called to say that Kim had made it through the long ordeal, though her heart had stopped twice during the operation. Her condition was critical, but she was still alive.

We were told they had been unable to save the baby, a girl. It appeared the baby had been killed on impact with the drunk driver. I felt a knot form in my throat at the thought that one man's drunken fun had now killed two children.

As Kim was being wheeled into the unit, we got a call from the other hospital where her mother and mother-in-law had been taken. Both women had died within the last hour. The death toll now reached five, including the unborn baby. I prayed we could save the young woman who had just lost most of her family.

The form that was brought in barely resembled a human. Kim had been wrapped from head to toe in white gauze and bandage. In the top of her skull was a device called an I.C.P., or inter-cranial pressure, screw. It measured the stress on the brain and gave us valuable information on her status.

There were small slits for her eyes, if she ever opened them again. A round opening, a tracheotomy, had been made in Kim's throat for the plastic tube that connected Kim to the life-supporting ventilator.

While making setting changes on the ventilator, I listened to the report given by the anesthesiologist and the surgeon. The prognosis wasn't good.

Kim was in a deep coma. The baby had been taken, her bones had been set, and plastic surgery had been performed on her ruined face. If she survived, many more procedures would follow, much of it plastic surgery. At this point, medical science had done all it could. It was now up to Kim, and her will to live, to keep her alive. I wondered at the courage that it would take to overcome such a horrible tragedy, and have the will to survive. From somewhere, she was going to have to find more strength than most of us would ever know. It came in the form of the man that walked into her room.

Kim's husband, Ron, stood there, his face as pale as the bandages covering his wife's body, and tears coursing down his handsome face. He turned his attention to me for only a moment, but long enough for me to see more raw pain than I've ever seen before. My heart went out to this distraught man, and I walked to him to place an arm around his shoulders.

"Ron, she's come a long way. We're all amazed at her progress. I won't lie to you. It's bad; it's very bad. But, if Kim is strong, if she can feel your love, she may just pull through this."

He cleared his throat, trying to talk around the constriction from crying.

"Yes, the doctor told me everything. He said she most likely wouldn't survive. But I've already lost enough, and he doesn't know my Kim. She'll do this. WE will do this."

I smiled and hoped he was right.

Ron dried his eyes and walked to the side of her bed.

"Kim? Honey, it's me. Ron. I'm here, baby. You be strong for me, you hear? God will get you through this honey, if you help Him. It's going to be tough, but with His help, we can make it."

Ron then knelt beside the bed and began to talk to God in Kim's behalf. I quietly left the room to stand outside the door and wipe my eyes. I bowed my own head for a moment and asked God to listen, and to let Ron keep his Kim. I was aware that He already knew, but I reminded God that this loving couple had already lost enough.

A few minutes after Ron left, Kim's heart stopped again. A "code" was called, and we worked feverishly to save her. It took almost an hour to stabilize her once again. The readings from the I.C.P. screw were rising alarmingly, and we worried she wouldn't survive much longer.

Kim made it through the rest of my shift, and I prayed for her on my way home. In fact, when I went to bed, I fell asleep praying for Kim.

When I went back to work the next night, I was happily surprised she was still with us. She was still in a coma, but showed signs of improvement that amazed her doctors.

One week after the accident, Kim moved a finger. That may not seem like much, but it filled our hearts with joy. She had also begun to respond to pain stimulus, a good sign. For the first time, we began to hope.

Two weeks after she was admitted, Kim developed pneumonia. Along with her broken body, she was fighting an infection that would be uncomfortable, but uneventful, in a relatively healthy person, yet one that may kill her. Several more bags were added to the IV stands surrounding her bed, more equipment brought into her already crowded room.

What small progress we noticed had diminished with the infection consuming Kim's lungs. We once again waited for Kim to die.

Unlike us, though, Ron Sanders never gave up, never wavered in his faith that God would pull Kim through. He sat by her bed for hours, praying out loud, showing no shame that he was heard.

Each time I saw his head bent, or heard his whispered pleas, my heart would hurt for him. I knew that God could rescue Kim, but I believe that everything has a season. I felt that it was Kim's time, that her season was over.

Ten days into the pneumonia, raging fever, and eventual seizures,

Kim showed a rapid improvement. So rapid, in fact, all of us were quite surprised. Still in a coma, Kim's condition was bumped back up to "stable", instead of "critical".

She seemed to rest comfortably, nestled in her cocoon of medication and bandages. No improvement, no digression, no change. It continued to be this way for another two months. Two months of Kim not responding, and two months of Ron praying at his wife's bedside. The gentle young man's unwavering faith never ceased to astound me. We, as medical staff that had seen the full spectrum of human misery and death, had given up, but not Ron. This determined man seemed to have the faith of ten men. A pain that would have broken most of us had forged a bond of steel between a comatose wife and loving husband.

Kim was in intensive care for two months before she was stable enough to be moved to a step-down, monitored floor. Though still in a coma, she was once again responding to pain stimulus and moving that one, small finger.

Once she was moved from the unit, Kim's improvement escalated. For some patients, just being surrounded by loved ones, out of the intensive care setting, can create wonder. And Kim was never alone. At any given time, you'd find her sister, brother, or father-in-law chatting to her. And though Kim was unable to answer, Ron seemed to be with her constantly, kissing her face, whispering his love into her ear. He had taken a leave of absence from the factory to be with Kim, and to make sure God didn't forget her.

Six months after the terrible tragedy, Kim awoke. I was fortunate enough to be on duty when she did. Ron was so excited, so filled with joy, it didn't take long for word to spread throughout the hospital that Kim's eyes were open.

I took a quick break just to rush to Kim's room, only to find a crowd both inside the room, and waiting in the hallway. The circumstances surrounding Kim's accident had affected all of us that had come into contact with her, and even those who hadn't. All of us wanted to witness this phenomenon first hand. It was one of those uplifting moments when I was thrilled to have been part of saving a life.

Ron sat on the side of Kim's bed, holding his wife's hand, his face wreathed in a joyous smile. He beamed at the praises given to Kim and the soft hugs he was given by the staff.

As I finally made it into the room, I heard Ron say, "Well, yes, she's done beautifully. And we know we have a long way to go, but we can do it. We also know that without God, none of this would have happened. Even when everyone else gave up, we knew that God would help us. And just look at the miracle He's given us."

Throughout the next few weeks, Kim steadily improved. She had a very long, very rough, road ahead of her. But I thought with Ron and God on her side, she would come full circle.

Eight months after she was first brought to us, Kim was taken off the ventilator forever. She was then moved to our rehabilitation unit in another building. I often went to visit Kim, though she, of course, didn't remember me. It didn't matter, I remembered her, and always would.

While in rehab, Kim had to be taught how to speak, eat, walk, and make decisions again. There were times when she would become frustrated, angry, and depressed, but none of us blamed her. If anyone ever had a right to become irritated, it was Kim. These episodes were few and far between, though. For the most part, Kim was more than cooperative, seeming to be inspired by her husband's loving devotion, and her abiding faith in a power higher than her own. To this day, I have met few people that have the strength that Kim Sanders had to overcome the most terrible things that could be inflicted on a human.

It has now been just over two years since Kim was brought into the hospital. Two years of waiting for her to die, then watching her climb the seemingly insurmountable mountain. Two years of listening to Ron talk to God, and two years of seeing the miracles that He gave the faithful, young couple in love.

Last month, Kim and Ron Sanders were granted one more miracle. Along with Kim's full, unbelievable recovery, they were given a perfect baby girl. The baby's name signifies all that is good in this world, the one thing that kept her mother alive. Her name is Hope.

Never Give Up

It's funny how people remember even the smallest detail of what they were doing when they first hear devastating news. Just like we all remember what were doing when we heard the news that President Kennedy had been assassinated. Most people even remember where they were when they first heard Elvis Presley had died. Usually mundane things stand out in sharp detail in our minds. Maybe it's the way our hearts try to cushion the blow.

Connie Wells was cleaning up the kitchen in the aftermath of breakfast with her husband and four children. It was her favorite time of the day. Early morning summer sun was winding its way lazily into the room, dancing across the floor and creating fanciful shadows on the walls. She could hear the happy songs of the birds outside and grinned when she heard Bailey's soft "woof" on the other side of the screen door, telling her it was time to come in for her own breakfast. It was one of those days when you're glad just to be alive, all is well in your world, and you couldn't possible imagine life being any better than it is right at that moment. A day when nothing bad is ever going to touch you, and you will be happy forever.

Then one phone call from a stranger turns your entire world upside down, and you can't imagine life ever being good again.

When the telephone rang, she automatically reached over and turned down the volume of the "oldies but goodies" radio program she had been listening to before she picked up the receiver. Anticipating the phone call she got every morning from her husband, she was smiling when she answered.

"Good morning!"

But it wasn't Jerry on the other end of the line. It was the grim, professional voice of someone she was yet to meet.

"Mrs. Wells?"

She began to feel cold, reaction to a yet unrealized fear, somehow knowing this was going to be bad news.

"Yes, this is Connie Wells."

"Mrs. Wells, this is Janie Thompson at Baptist Hospital. I'm calling you from the ER. Mrs. Wells, your son, David, was just brought in by EMSA. He had an accident at work, and was transported here."

"But, but... What happened? Is he all right? I don't understand..."

"Mrs. Wells, the doctor will give you all the details when you get here. All I can tell you is that David fell at work and injured his head. I'm sorry, but those are all the details I have at this time. We have been trying to contact your husband, but we don't have his work number. Would you like me to call him for you? The doctor wants both of you to come in."

"No. Uh...I can call Jerry... Is this serious? How bad is it?"

"Mrs. Wells, as I said, I have no further details. The doctor has asked me to tell you and Mr. Wells to come in as soon as possible. Are you all right to drive? Should I call someone to drive you in?"

"No, I'll be okay. I'll call my husband and we'll be there immediately."

Her hands were trembling so badly she punched numbers on the phone four times before she got Jerry's office.

"Jerry Wells. How may I help you?"

"Jerry?" Her voice broke. "Jerry, something's happened to David! He's in the emergency room at Baptist Hospital. They won't tell me what happened, but just said the doctor wants us there as soon as possible."

Jerry didn't waste time asking questions for which she had no answers.

"Honey, I'll be right there to pick you up. It will only be a few minutes. Stay calm, Sweetheart. It's probably nothing serious. David will be just fine. See you in a few minutes, Connie."

45

She began to pace the floor, feeling the pulse throbbing at her throat. She toyed with the canisters on the counter top, moving them around, then returning them to their original positions next to the toaster. She turned off the coffeepot, then folded and refolded the dishtowel. Then she noticed she was doing nothing, merely standing in the middle of her sun-dappled kitchen, staring into space. She jerked with the realization she needed to comb her hair and put on her shoes. It was if her mind was moving in slow motion, yet was spinning dizzily out of control.

Connie was out the door and running to the car even before Jerry was in the driveway. His face was as pale as she felt. He offered her a tight smile for reassurance, grabbed her hand and held it as he drove.

They broke all the speed limits along the way. She didn't think either of them cared if the police stopped them. In fact, they may have welcomed it, hoping they would escort them to the hospital with lights and sirens. She felt as if they just couldn't seem to get there fast enough.

The fourteen story building loomed in front of them, waiting, and her feeling of doom was more pronounced, made somehow more concrete by the gray stone of the hospital.

Jerry parked the car at an awkward angle in the parking space. When he got out, he saw the sloppy job he'd done and moved to unlock the door and rearrange the car's position. Connie looked at him with her mouth open and her eyebrows risen into surprised peaks that he would dare to take time to move the car. Jerry paused at her attention, then moved with a jerk to the back of the car, putting his keys back into his pocket so savagely, he ripped the seam of his pants.

The automatic doors whispered open at their arrival. Outside, the air was filled with the sounds of birds singing. Inside, it was pandemonium. It seemed as if the waiting room was overflowing with the sick, both real and imagined. As they impatiently waited to speak to someone, anyone, Connie noticed some of the patients were wheezing for breath, while others sat nursing what appeared to be very minor injuries that could have been handled at any doctor's office. A pretty nurse that asked if she could help them drew her gaze away.

Jerry's voice trembled, "Our son...we, uh...received a call from someone...I'm sorry, I don't know who called." He turned to his wife, hurt bewilderment on his face, "Connie? What was that woman's name? The one that called you awhile ago?"

Connie had reached the end of her limits. "I don't remember her name. She called and told me my son was here, and I want to see him. His name is David." Her voice grew soft, husky. "David Alan Wells. Where is he? Where's my son? What happened? For God's sake, why won't someone tell me what's wrong with him?"

"Come with me, Mr. and Mrs. Wells. I'll take you to the lounge. The doctor is in the room with David now, and he'll answer all your questions. I'll go in and tell him you're here."

When the nurse informed me the Wells were waiting, I finished writing in the chart and walked out of the trauma room. As the attending physician, I've dealt with a great deal of grief in the emergency department, yet it never fails to astound me how life's twists and turns can destroy a family so quickly. This was going to be another one of those heart-breaking cases that I would take to the grave with me.

David Wells, age 18, one month past high school graduation, had just started a new job. In fact, it was his first day at work, and only three hours into the shift. His supervisor was training him when a sharp piece of metal had nicked his finger. It wasn't a large cut, more like a scrape really, but it had begun to bleed. The supervisor had wrapped a napkin around it, told David to go to the washroom and rinse it off while he got the first aid kit.

David was standing in front of the sink, cold water pouring over the finger that was still bleeding slightly, his face ashen beneath the fluorescent lights of the washroom. The supervisor, concerned, asked if he was feeling all right.

David had grinned, "Aw, I don't do well with the sight of blood. Good thing I'm going to study computers in college and not medicine, huh?" The smile had just started to slide from his face when David passed out. Before his supervisor could reach him, David fell and hit his head on the edge of the porcelain sink, then fell to the floor. Alarmed, the supervisor yelled for some help and told someone to call an ambulance.

When the paramedics arrived, David had stopped breathing and they couldn't detect a heart beat. They knelt on the cold tile and began CPR, at last being rewarded with an acceptable cardiac and respiratory rhythm. While the patient was stable, they immobilized him on the stretcher and raced to the ambulance.

Enroute, the EMT with David noticed the cardiac rhythms on the monitor were becoming irregular. He told the driver to pick up the speed before they had to "code" this kid again, when the monitor alarms went off, signaling that the patient was asystole, or "flat-line". The EMT began to administer one-man CPR while the driver switched to the "high-low" mode siren, sounding much like the ambulances in Europe. This was the siren drivers heard when they didn't clear the street fast enough and the patient was very critical. The sound echoed back from the surrounding buildings, announcing this was a life or death situation.

Traffic parted and the ambulance driver took the opening through the middle of four lanes of traffic. The hospital was at last in sight when David's heart picked up a static rhythm and he began to breathe, shallowly, on his own once again.

I stood waiting for them as they rushed into the room. I spoke with the paramedic while they were still removing the restraints that held the young man. Like all medical staff adept at their job, they gave a comprehensive report while still working.

"David Wells, age 18, injured at work. Evidently, he fell, hit his head on the bathroom sink, and was immediately unconscious. Upon arrival, we found the patient without vital signs of any kind. We started CPR and got a sinus tach rhythm, then placed him in the ambulance. Enroute, he went asystole again, and CPR was done until we were just down the street, and he began to pick up on his own. He's intubated with a seven point five endotrachial tube and breath sounds are equal and bilateral. B/P is now ninety over sixty, respirations are eight to ten.."

"Doctor James?" One of the nurses came into the room. "The Wells just got here. They want to speak to you. I put them in the lounge and told them you'd be out soon."

Knowing that the parents were probably worried and scared, I did a quick assessment of David before ordering a CAT scan to see what his brain looked like. Respiratory Therapy was setting up the ventilator and the nurse was drawing blood as I left the exam room.

Connie and Jerry Wells both stood when I entered the room. Their faces were almost as pasty white as their son's. Connie held her purse, twisting and bending the strap till it looked as if it would break. Jerry's eyes were large and round, and his bottom lip trembled. I introduced myself as I shook their hands.

"Mr. and Mrs. Wells, my name is Dr. James. I'm the attending physician for the ER today. I haven't had time to do a full evaluation of David yet. I've ordered several tests and will know more later. But from what I've seen so far, it would appear that David sustained a hard blow to the front of his head, knocking him out. He fell while at work and hit a sink. His heart has stopped twice, and CPR was done to get him back."

Connie's quick intake of breath betrayed the calmness she was trying to present. Jerry's eyes began to water, and one teardrop slipped down his cheek. He was the first to speak.

"How bad is it, Doc?"

"Jerry, I just can't answer that until I have test results back. I know you're very upset, and I don't blame you. All I ask is that you give us a chance to check him out, and I'll come back and talk to you the second I have anything to report. Okay?"

Connie nodded numbly and Jerry just stared back at me. As I left the lounge, I felt as if the entire weight of the world was on my shoulders. I hoped I could give them good news later.

But good news wasn't in the cards for David. The CAT scan revealed a rather large cranial bleed that was putting pressure on the brain. He was no longer breathing on his own, so the ventilator was his only life support. We gave IV drugs to keep his heart pumping.

From the test results I had so far, the prognosis wasn't good. I walked back to the lounge more discouraged than I could allow to show.

Again, the Wells stood at my arrival. Coffee cups and Connie's lack of shoes demonstrated just how long they'd been waiting.

"Jerry? Connie? It doesn't look good. There is massive bleeding in David's brain. There is quite a bit of pressure building up, and I'm afraid I'm going to have to call in a surgeon. If we don't operate, he's not going to make it."

Jerry cleared his throat, but his voice was still husky. "And if you do operate...then what? He'll be okay then? I mean, after he gets over the surgery. Then, he'll be alright?"

Connie's eyes shined with unshed tears and her face was filled with cautious hope.

"I just don't know, I truly don't. Let's get through surgery and see where we stand, okay? I wish there was more I could offer you now, but this is it. There is a phone over on the table, if you'd like to call anyone to come stay with you. I'm going to get a surgeon in here right away, so David should be going into surgery in less than an hour. I'll be back as soon as I can." They remained silent, but I heard Connie's sob as I shut the door to the lounge.

Surgery was fast and furious. The operating physician told me later that he found a mess when he got into David's brain. To make matters worse, the operating team had to stop during surgery to do CPR one more time.

I spoke with the surgeon after it was all over and the news was grim.

"I think you should probably order an EEG just to see if there are any brain waves going on. I hate to say this, but I think you'll probably get either a slow reading, or no reading at all. That boy is in serious trouble, and I don't think he's going to come out of it."

I nodded in agreement while I looked over the x-rays taken before, during, and after the operation. Yes, I knew that David was in bad shape. I picked up the phone and ordered a STAT EEG. Then I sank wearily onto a chair to catch my breath and wait for the test results.

David had been sent to a room in our surgical intensive care unit.

While he was still being transported, I found the Wells to escort them to the waiting room on the floor where their son was "resting". I spoke with them on the elevator since we were alone and it wasn't a betrayal of patient confidentiality. I admitted to them that it wasn't looking good for a complete recovery, but I held back most of the information until I could get a reading on the EEG.

After I settled them into the waiting room, I went to David's room. The EEG technician was already there and I could see a thin strip of paper being ejected from the machine. I was trained enough to see that the lines on the graph weren't those compatible with life. I suddenly noticed I had an excruciating headache.

The technician looked at me, glanced down at the graph, then back into my face. She just shook her head; no further words were needed. I turned and left the room.

Even though tiredness was etched into their faces, the Wells again stood when I came into the room. This seems to be a common practice when a patient's family sees the physician come in. Both of them had hope in their eyes, but I could see it slip away as they stared into my face. To be honest, I didn't try to hide the misery on mine. I wanted my face to begin to prepare them for the news I was being forced to give them.

Connie sank to the chair and Jerry leaned over to touch her hair, but still looking into my eyes. I could see the rest of the color of his face seep away with each passing second.

"He's dead, isn't he, Dr. James?"

"No, Jerry, he's still alive, or what you may consider still alive. The trauma to his brain was bad. The damage it did was irreversible."

Connie was openly crying now and her words were hard to understand.

"So, what you're telling us, David is, for all intents and purposes, dead."

"Connie...Jerry... God, I hate to say this. We had an EEG done on him to check for brain activity. I'm afraid it showed very little brain waves. I'm so sorry..."

Connie jumped from her chair, her eyes suddenly dry and

somehow wild. "I want to see him! I want to go to David now. I want to touch him, tell him I love him. I want to..."

Jerry began to cry, not bothering to try to look brave any longer. His wife's words had cut to the chase.

I took them to David's room and heard the loud gasp as they saw him connected to machines of all kinds. They stood on opposite sides of the bed, holding his hand, and whispering into his ear. They told him how much they loved him, how proud they were of him, how they were praying for him.

They stared at the various monitors, trying to decipher what all of it meant. They watched the rhythmic lines flash across the screens, and it all must have appeared normal to them, because their next words floored me.

"David is going to be okay, Jerry."

"Yes honey, I know that. I can feel it, too."

As much as I could appreciate their loving hope, I felt honor-bound to let them see how futile their hope was. I wanted to tell them that all the prayers in the world wouldn't save David, wouldn't make him wake up, wouldn't allow him to be the same young man that had left the house that morning.

"Connie; Jerry. I know you're upset. I know you're heartbroken. I feel, though, that you're refusing to accept the truth here. David isn't going to wake up. His medical status isn't going to change. I don't mean to be cruel, I just hate to see you harbor false hope."

Connie smiled for the first time since I'd met her. "Oh, it's not false hope, Doctor. Believe me, it's very real."

Jerry nodded in agreement again, also smiling.

"I realize this is hard to take in right now. I'll go and give you time to work this out. One other thing I'd like to mention, though it bothers me to do so at this time. If you should choose to remove life support, I'll be here to take care of it for you. Please think about what I've told you. Really think about it."

Jerry, for the first time, showed anger. "No! No, we will not think about it, because he's going to be fine. And don't start about donating organs, either! I know that's where you're going next, and we refuse to allow that! You see, we believe there is a higher power than you. We believe that miracles happen every day, and it's going to happen to David."

I smiled though my heart was aching for them. I patted them on the back and walked from the room. Behind me, the machines hummed.

I went to the doctor's lounge and fell upon one of the sofas. It was the last thing I remembered until my pager went off at 5 AM the next morning. I stumbled to the phone, wiping sleep from my red eyes.

"This is Dr. James."

"Doctor, I think you should get down here to the unit. David Wells is starting to move, and his parents are singing!"

As I ran to the elevator, I could feel my head aching. I didn't know what was happening, but I knew that David Wells was not going to wake up and go home like his parents believed he would.

Fewer things have shocked me more than seeing David open his eyes when I said his name. Not only did he open them, they were sparkling! He attempted to smile around the tube in his mouth, and I'm sure it was at my look of astonishment.

I yelled for the nurse to get another STAT EEG, and only then noticed that Connie and Jerry were, indeed, singing. They were singing one of my grandmother's favorite hymns, "Rock of Ages", and they were laughing.

The graph that the machine put out was alive with brain waves. I could feel my face flush and my own eyes widen. Connie and Jerry didn't have to have a medical degree to understand what it meant. They began to sing just a little louder, and continued to smile at me. I've never been so happy to be wrong in my life.

It was a hard battle for David after he was taken off the ventilator. He had to learn to walk and talk all over again. But it was worth the wait because that boy could talk a blue streak!

He was in rehabilitation for almost six months, working so hard that his therapists had to force him to slow down and rest. It never ceased to amaze me at his tenacity, his iron will, to get on with his life.

Last month I received an invitation in the mail as I have from several patients. Usually, I didn't attend whatever function was being announced, but I wouldn't have missed this one for the world.

Tonight, I watched David Wells walk across the stage and receive his college diploma. It seemed that everyone in the auditorium was familiar with his story, because as he took the parchment into his hand, a thunderous applause washed over the room. I have to admit, I was the first one on my feet, standing for an ovation to a very determined, very loved young man.

The Promise of Spring

Gray clouds blotted out the world that was being deluged with a mid-January rain. Jessie had the defroster turned on high, trying to dispel the haze that stubbornly clung to the windshield. It had already been a long, miserable day, now the drive home was going to be lousy, too. As he drove, Jessie tried to force himself to think cheerful, sunny thoughts. It wasn't too difficult a task...he thought about Kim.

In his mind, he could envision her bright, happy smile, her lovely face that reflected the love she had for her new husband of just three weeks. He could feel her hands lovingly stroking his forehead while he reclined in his chair after a hard day at work, much like today. He was already looking forward to opening the door and being greeted by his beautiful blonde bride. Anxious to see her, he pressed harder on the accelerator. He grinned into the gloom, barely noticing how heavy the traffic was becoming.

Jessie became irritated that the old truck's defroster wasn't working like it should. Visibility was bad due to the heavy condensation on the glass. He fumbled around the seat next to him until he found a paper towel. Leaning over the steering wheel, he began to rub the paper back and forth across the damp glass, trying vainly to clear a spot he could see through.

At that moment, the cell phone lying next to him began to ring. Jessie was sure it was his wife, anxious to speak to him. He smiled as he reached for the phone, hit the button that opened the connection between himself and Kim, when he lost control of the truck.

A woman in a car coming from the opposite direction could see the handsome young man wiping at his windshield. She then saw the young man veering into the other lane, straight into oncoming traffic. She saw this all unfolding, but was helpless to stop the accident that followed. She later told me that it felt as if she had stopped breathing, so intense was her reaction to what was happening two cars ahead of her.

The sound of colliding metal and breaking glass was heard for several city blocks. The semi-truck that Jessie hit sustained little damage. On the other hand, Jessie's pick-up truck was demolished in the collision. The only thing that saved Jessie's life was being thrown through the windshield at the moment of impact. He slammed into an oak tree, his body traveling in excess of seventy miles an hour, and hit headfirst. Surviving an accident such at this isn't always good. So severe was the injury, Jessie was immediately plunged into a deep coma. On the other end of the cell phone's connection, Kim Connelly heard the crash.

The female witness was dialing 911 on her cell phone even before the sounds of the accident stopped echoing in her ears. She was so nervous, her voice was barely audible when the operator asked what type of assistance she needed. When asked her location, she became confused and had to get the driver of the car behind her to get on the phone and give directions.

A crowd quickly gathered around the prone body lying at the base of the tree. Two of the motorists stood in the road, directing traffic. The driver of the semi-truck knelt beside Jessie, put his hands over his face and cried. The line of cars stopped for the accident grew longer.

I was at the end of that line. I pulled my car as close to the side of the road as I could manage, then stepped from the car. I walked quickly toward the accident to offer my assistance as a paramedic. I had no idea what I would find when I got there.

Only from the build of the body could I surmise this was a young man. I couldn't tell from his face or hands because they were almost totally obliterated. It was obvious that the victim had had time to throw his hands in front of his face to try to protect himself, though it had been a futile gesture.

The injury to the palms of his callused hands was minimal compared to those of his face. Not even this man's mother could have recognized him at this point. If he survived, if he was even still alive at this moment, he would need extensive plastic surgery in an attempt to make his face human again.

My heart felt as if it were being squeezed by the emotions I was feeling. I pushed that aside to run the last few feet to the man lying so still on the ground, his face turned up into the downpour of rain. Someone was next to him, seeming about to move his body.

"No! Don't move him!"

"But he's lying in the rain, Lady. I just want to get him out of the rain. I was being careful."

"I understand, but you cannot move him. Someone get an umbrella to hold over him. I'm sorry, I didn't mean to yell. I don't want you to paralyze him or finish killing him by moving him."

"Are you a doctor, lady?"

"No, I'm a paramedic. Will everyone please step back? Has anyone called for an ambulance?"

A woman next to me spoke up, her voice choking on sobs.

"Yes, I did. I called for one right after it happened. They should be here any second."

As if on cue, I then heard the rapidly approaching sound of a siren. I had a moment to think that even on my day off-duty, I was going to be putting a patient into the back of one of our units.

The ambulance stopped in the middle of the street, the siren was switched off, and the sudden silence seemed deafening. My best friend, Neil, stepped from the ambulance. I smiled when I saw him, and the corners of his mouth lifted when he saw me.

"Hey Rhonda, whatcha got here? Heck of a way to spend our days off, huh?"

"Auto accident, young man as far as I can tell. I haven't had time to get the vitals. You guys got here fast."

"Yeah, well, we were just down the street grabbing something to eat when the call came in. And I thought working overtime was going to be quiet today. I should've known better with all this rain."

Neil knelt beside the patient, the pants of his uniform getting as saturated as his shirt already was. Rainwater gathered on the lens of his glasses, and he flicked it off without thought, reacting instinctually to the situation before him. I knelt beside him, opening the large box at our side, working in a habitual rhythm as long-time partners do.

Using the stethoscope, I listened to breath sounds and determined the patient's right lung was near collapse. I pulled a plastic oxygen mask from the box and connected the tubing to the portable E-tank. The face trauma was so massive, I held the mask as close as possible, not daring to place it on the destroyed face. Neil cut the man's shirt away to place EKG leads on his chest, then watched the read-out on the monitor. Possibly the only good news at this point was a fairly regular sinus rhythm on the printout sheet Neil handed me to see.

The patient assessment that Neil did was quick and efficient. He relayed information into the phone that was linked to the closest hospital in Rochester. His voice was crisp, professional, giving all pertinent details as he continued to work.

I helped Neil and the attending EMT to get the young man onto a backboard, moving him carefully to avoid possible further injury to his spine. We pulled the straps tight to hold him securely. Neil then asked if I'd like to accompany them to the hospital, since I had been the one to initiate medical aide. I told him I'd follow in my own car, as soon as I could wind my way through the traffic snarl that had developed.

It was as I was walking back to my car that I found the woman that had called for an ambulance. She was lying across the hood of her car, her head resting on her crossed arms as she sobbed. I laid my hand on her back, and she turned to me to be comforted. She began to talk rapidly, almost babbling at times, about how the accident had affected her. I assured her she had done everything possible, and thanked her for getting help there so quickly. Her tears began to subside, and she smiled at me.

"How can you, as a woman, do this work?"

"I do it to help other people. I can't imagine doing anything else."

The ER was busy when I arrived. The rain had caused several accidents, and it seemed as if all the victims had been brought here.

I saw Neil in one of the exam rooms, giving his report to the attending physician, Dr. Fielding.

Radiology was there; taking shots from every possible angle. I overheard the doctor telling Neil that a plastic surgeon was on his way to look at the patient. I also heard that the patient now had a name.

"Jessie Connelly, age 24. He lives about 20 minutes from here." The nurse pulled a small white card from one of the plastic windows of the wallet. She smiled sadly.

"It's a card used to send out with wedding announcements. Oh Lord, he's been married for less than a month. I guess I need to call his wife." She walked slowly from the exam room, and sighed deeply as she dialed the number.

"Mrs. Connelly? This is Mary with County General Medical Center. Mrs. Connelly, I'm sorry to inform you that there's been an accident. Your husband is here, in the Emergency Department, being treated now."

A short pause, during which Mary's mouth turned down at the corners. It was obvious she was upset about the call she had to make.

"No dear, I don't really know the extent of his injuries at this time. The doctor is still in with him. Perhaps you should get someone to drive you here. Maybe Jessie's parents? Yes, I think that's a good idea, honey. We'll see you in just a little while. Please try to be calm, Kim. We're going to do our very best to help your husband."

Mary silently replaced the phone and I saw the glimmer of tears in her eyes. She felt my gaze and tried to smile.

"Well, no one ever said life is fair, did they?"

She walked back into the examination room to help the attending physician.

I saw a technician wheeling in machinery. From the appearance, I recognized it as an EEG machine, to test brain activity. I mentally crossed my fingers.

Kim Connelly must have urged her in-laws to drive like the wind. They arrived before I had finished filling out my report. To be honest, I was dragging my feet just a bit, wanting to see what the EEG report had said.

Kim was about to push the door open to the examination room when Dr. Fielding came out to meet her.

He put his arm around her trembling shoulders, and I immediately knew it was bad. He looked toward Jessie's parents, and they quickly walked over to him.

"Folks, I'm sorry…"

Kim started to moan and sway on her feet. Jessie's mother held her fist to her open mouth, trying hard to not cry out loud. Her husband's face was drained of all color. Dr. Fielding spoke rapidly, to stem the approaching hysteria we all sensed.

"Wait, you don't understand. Jessie is still alive."

All three family members went through an amazing metamorphosis right before our eyes. All they had heard was the word "alive". I knew that wasn't the whole story. Dr. Fielding went on with his diagnosis.

"Please, listen to me carefully now. While he is still alive, he's definitely in serious trouble. The EEG, or electroencephalograph, shows minimal brain activity. What that means is that Jessie is in a deep coma, and may or may not recover from the head injuries he suffered."

The relative calm that had transcended was disappearing with the grief that walked into the room with the family. They began to ask questions in hushed tones, as if they didn't dare to lift their voices for fear the peace would shatter at their feet.

Dr. Fielding was kind, but he was firm. In a no-nonsense tone, he told them that Jessie might never awaken. If he did, he may be partially paralyzed, or have brain damage. I saw a family that would love, accept, and care for Jessie, no matter what the outcome. I was struck by their loving devotion.

Dr. Fielding then told them he was keeping Jessie heavily sedated even though he was comatose, to allow the swelling in the brain to subside. It was his fervent wish that Jessie not go to surgery.

"I'm sorry, folks. At this point, it's really a 'wait and see' situation. There is no way to rush this, and there is no way to tell you the outcome. I can only give you educated guesses. In my opinion, and I wish I could give you more hope, it doesn't look good. I'm afraid Jessie may never wake up. If he does, then we'll deal with what comes next."

For the first time, I heard Kim Connelly's voice...loud, strong, and true.

"It doesn't matter what happens *if* Jessie wakes up. The only important thing is that he *does* wake up. We'll deal with whatever happens. I married him for better, for worse, in sickness and in health. I think that pretty much covers this, don't you? We'll be here for him, for as long as it takes." Her eyes were sad though her lips were smiling.

It was to be a tough road to travel for Kim, Jessie's parents, for all of them. Most of the time, Jessie was surrounded by loving friends and relatives, urging him to wake up and come home.

Jessie developed several different infections, with most of them seeming to affect his lungs. He would have a temperature, and the next thing anyone knew, he was back on a ventilator again. During the next three months, Jessie was on a ventilator five times.

Breathing treatments were given every two hours to try to stave off pneumonia which could lead to certain death in Jessie's weakened condition. In fact, it was one of the respiratory care practitioners that announced the good news to everyone. In a way, it was humorous, though no one was laughing at the time.

The RCP's name was Angie. She worked the same area of the hospital every night on the 11-7 shift. She had been Jessie's therapist for over a month. As was her routine, she went into Jessie's room; told him her name as she did every night she worked, then explained the treatment she was starting. Angie felt the same way most medical staff does...we're just not sure how much a comatose patient actually understands about what is happening to him, or around him.

"Hello there, Jessie! It's me again, Angie. Honey, I'm going to start your breathing treatment now. I'm going to put this mask on your face and you'll feel a cool mist that has medicine in it."

Angie began to assemble her equipment when Jessie opened his eyes, look straight at her and said, "Hi there. How are you?" Angie dropped everything in her hands, plastic tubing falling to the floor in a heap.

"Uh, Jessie? I'm just fine. How are you, honey?"

Jessie smiled, "Oh, not too bad, I guess." Then he closed his eyes, sleeping rather than slipping back to the coma he had been immersed in for over three months. Angie smiled nervously, not sure whether to wake him or not, to tell him she'd be right back. She decided to just walk quickly, quietly, out the door. She practically ran to the nurses' station three rooms down the hall.

"Hey! Jessie's home, Jessie's home!"

The charge nurse looked at Angie as if she had lost her mind. "What are you talking about, girl? That boy's in a coma. 'Home', my foot!"

Angie was laughing and talking at the same time.

"Honest he is! He talked to me! He asked me how I am. Really, I'm not lying to you! Come on, I'll show you!"

The nurses' station was deserted as the entire floor staff walked with Angie to Jessie's room. The story of the young groom and his lovely, devoted wife had touched their hearts. They all held their breath in happy anticipation, hoping Angie hadn't imagined the whole episode.

Angie stood by Jessie's bed, took his hand in her own, and spoke to him as she had almost every night for over a month.

"Jessie? Hi, it's me again, Angie. There are some people here that would like to speak with you, Jessie."

Jessie's eyes remained closed and his breathing even, as he had been for the last few weeks. He was resting well, and it didn't seem he was about to talk to them. Angie's shoulders began to sag. The charge nurse was upset that the technician had gotten their hopes up that way.

"I knew it. Angie, you just *think* you heard him speak. You need a break, girl. Go down the hall, have a seat, take a deep breath and relax. It's okay, though, Angie. We all wanted it to be true."

Angie began to plead then. "Please, Jessie! Please open your eyes and speak to them. They don't believe me, Jessie. Please?"

The group of nurses and aides turned to leave the room. Some were looking at Angie with pity at her foolish hope. Others appeared angry with her. Angie's eyes filled with tears as she began to follow them from the room.

Behind them, they all heard a soft chuckle, and as one, they spun around to look at the pale young man lying on the bed.

Jessie grinned at them. "Hey! Where's everyone going?"

I only hope he wasn't startled by the happy laughter and excited voices that greeted his awakening after three months of dark exile. Through it all, he grinned, then asked them to call his wife.

Kim and Jessie's entire family arrived at the hospital around 3 AM. The room was filled with happy laughter, hugs and kisses.

Through subsequent testing, we found out that Jessie was going to be just fine. He would have to have extensive physical therapy to exercise his atrophied muscles, but he was young and strong. He could now do anything he had the determination to accomplish.

Jessie and Kim are now the proud parents of twin sons. Jessie opened his own business working with computers. From time to time, they stop in to visit the nurses and to thank the staff for all they did. And the doctors tell him, "Jessie, all it took was a little faith, a little will-power, and a lot of love."

Miniature Blessings

Diane sank, heavily, onto the soft cushions of the couch. Weariness and dejection were etched into her young face. A lovely face, so recently unlined by worry, shouldn't look so anxious. The soft-soled shoes she wore bit into the swollen flesh, and her gray face was puffy. With a sigh that seemed to come from the depths of her tired heart, she leaned back, supporting her rounded stomach with her small hands.

Diane's usually perpetual smile slipped just a notch, "Whew! I'm already worn out, and it's still morning!"

Struggling to get back on her feet, she asked, "Mom, you want some coffee? If you do, I'll go to the kitchen and start a pot."

Quickly I stood, and gently pushed her back down on the sofa, "No, honey. I'll make you some, though, if you want it. Or, I could fix you something to eat. What d'ya say?"

Ruefully, she smiled, "No thanks, Mom. I'm not thirsty, or hungry. Only tired."

Diane's advanced pregnancy of twenty-seven weeks was the main reason for her exhaustion. The other one was on the other side of the room, jumping up and down in his playpen.

As I watched him, I was struck by the beauty of the sunlight casting golden glints through his soft curls, and his big blue eyes dancing with happiness. He saw me looking at him and held out one pudgy baby hand, reaching for me, while holding onto the top of the playpen with the other, balancing his wobbly stance.

I grinned at this newest love of my life as I walked across the room,

"Hi there, Christopher! You look as if you want your grandma to hold you. Are you getting tired? Come on, Sweetie, let's go sit in the rocking chair. Granny's going to rock a little wild boy to sleep, even though he doesn't know that yet."

Grinning and gurgling in happy agreement to something that he would try to beg out of, if he could talk, Christopher clapped his hands in baby joy, falling on his rounded diaper-padded bottom.

I carried eleven-month-old Christopher back to the comfortable rocking chair, and settled him into the lap that was made to cuddle babies, and he grinned into my eyes. All the love in my heart threatened to spill over in loving tears that only grandmother can understand.

I began to slowly rock the squirming little body, while Christopher patted my open mouth, trying to entice me to make the "WA WA WA" sounds he liked to giggle over. I allowed this routine to go on for a few minutes until my mouth began to suffer, then I pulled his hand down, after kissing the wet, sweet smelling palm.

Understanding that his grandmother was tired of the game, Christopher patted his own mouth, laughing at his own type of sounds, wet from teething. The baby version of "WA WA WA", accompanied by the soothing rocking of the chair, became a rhythmic cadence to lull a fidgeting little boy to sleep.

Soon, his clear blue eyes drifted to a close, and his long eyelashes rested on his pink cheeks. I kept rocking, gazing at the wonder of this beautiful baby in my arms.

But Christopher wasn't going to be the baby for long. In just a matter of weeks, there was going to be quite an addition to his family. Diane was expecting twins! We were all amazed, since there have never been a multiple birth on either side of our families.

The prospect of twins wasn't something Diane was exactly happy about. She had said she was going to wait for at least a year after the first baby, to spend time with Christopher, and let her body recuperate. But, she made a mistake, and became pregnant. The idea of twins still took her by surprise. It was just another curve life had thrown her that she would deal with in her own, accepting way.

When I was still attending medical classes and my daughter had been a small girl, she began talking about having babies. It was hard for her to understand that she had to wait until she was grown, and married to the loving father of all those babies she so wanted to have.

For as long as I could remember, Diane had always said she wanted a lot of children, maybe six of them! A little girl doesn't realize what an enormous responsibility, both financial and emotional, that can put on a young couple. By the time she was nine years old, I had convinced her she had to first finish school, grow up, then find a decent man to marry, so she could start on her family.

Diane loved children. Oh, I know most people do, but for her, it was almost spiritual. Diane may have had to wait for her own kids, but she found a way to surround herself with children. For several months, while still in high school, she had volunteered at one of the childcare centers in our town, just to be around small children. I had always called her my "Mother Earth", and if anyone could have a large family, and be perfectly content, it would be her.

Seeing her now, half reclining on the sofa, streaks of fatigue stroking her face, I wondered if she still felt the same way.

Jim, the father of the rapidly expanding family, was outside, changing the oil and spark plugs in the family van. My husband, Al, was also outside, supervising, as usual.

The purpose of this impromptu tune-up of the car was the long trip ahead for Jim, Diane, and Christopher. They had come to visit us in Oklahoma, from our hometown in Tennessee, which was hundreds of miles away. They had wanted to visit us for several months and felt it would be a good idea to do it now, since they didn't want to travel closer to Diane's due date.

While the men worked on the van, Diane and I had spent the day doing laundry, helping pack their things back into the van, and running after Christopher. The strain was starting to show on my daughter.

While Christopher took his nap, I encouraged Diane to lie down. She insisted she couldn't sleep, so she might as well finish folding the clothes to put in the last of the suitcases.

Jim and Diane had decided to travel at night so Christopher would sleep most of the trip, and give Mom and Dad a break. Diane would drive the first part of the journey, with Jim taking over when she became tired. Judging by the way that she looked, I thought Jim might be driving quite early.

I went to the kitchen to start dinner. I wanted them to eat before they left so they wouldn't have to make so many stops along the way. I had also prepared them a few sandwiches and snacks to store behind one of the seats.

Al and Jim walked noisily back into the house when they finished, waking Christopher long before dinner was ready. Jim washed his hands and picked up the baby, since Diane was still carrying clothes to the bedroom where the suitcases were lying open on the bed.

The only one that showed any enthusiasm for food was Al. Jim was tired, Christopher was fussy, and Diane didn't seem to have much of an appetite. I was already missing them, and dreaded seeing them leave so badly, I wasn't hungry, either.

When the dinner was over, Jim and Al carried the last of the luggage to the van. Diane was sitting in the recliner and I was holding Christopher in my lap, kissing his face, and telling him how much I was going to miss him.

I was so concerned about Diane, and told her that maybe they should wait until the next morning to leave.

"I wish we could, Mom, but we can't. Jim has to get back to work, and we're cutting it close as it is. I just dread this trip so badly. I don't feel too well. My back hurts and I thought it looked like I'm spotting blood."

Alarm made my heart race, "Diane? Honey, do you really think you should leave? Maybe you should call a doctor."

She shook her head, "Oh, I'll be alright, Mom. I did this when I was carrying Christopher, and my doctor said I might do it again. I'm only twenty-seven weeks, so I don't think it's anything serious. I'll be okay."

I walked over to sit beside her on the couch, "Sweetheart, are you sure? I mean, I know Jim has to get back to work, but this is more important. Surely his boss would understand if he was a day late, if it might endanger the twins."

Diane leaned her head on my shoulder, just as she had when she was a little girl, "No, Mom, I'm okay. Once we get on the road, and Christopher goes to sleep, I'll let Jim drive and I'll rest."

At the look on my face, she wanted to reassure me, and she smiled, "I promise, Mom, I'll be okay."

It was to be a promise Diane wouldn't be able to keep.

The van was loaded much too quickly, and Jim came back into the house to collect his presently still-small family. He reached down to take Christopher from my arms, and Christopher hung onto me, as if he understood they were leaving.

I hugged his little body to me, kissed his face, and told him to be a good boy, all the while trying to not let him know I was crying.

Al and I walked them outside to the driveway and Jim leaned over to kiss my cheek.

"See ya, Mom. I love you."

With tears now running freely down my face, I said, "I love you, too, Jim. Be careful. Take care of Christopher, and *my* baby, Diane. You have a very precious cargo here, Jim. Don't forget that."

As Jim was putting Christopher in the car seat, I took Diane in my arms. I always hated to see her leave, feeling as if my heart would break when she pulled out of the driveway, but this time was worse. I don't know if it was some sort of premonition, but I didn't want her to leave. Not then.

"I love you, Diane. I love you with all my heart. I still wish you'd think about staying until tomorrow, but I know you won't. Take care of you and those little people you're carrying. I'm going to miss you so much."

She was crying so hard she had trouble speaking, "I love you, too, Mom. Oh, I hate to go. I love coming to see you, but the minute I get here, I start dreading the time I have to leave. I'll be careful. I love you."

Diane kissed her stepfather goodbye, and told him to take care of her mother. Jim shook Al's hand before he climbed into the passenger seat.

I didn't sleep too well that night, and because of it, Al didn't, either.

When I'm restless, I toss and turn, and my poor husband got up for work almost as tired as when he went to bed.

After Al left, I started getting my books together for the class I was taking at the local junior college. I had two major tests that day, but I was certain I wasn't going to be able to concentrate on them.

As I left, I made sure the answering machine was turned on, so that Diane could leave a message, telling me that they had arrived safely.

As soon as I got home after school, I rushed to the answering machine. My eyes grew large when I saw there was no message from my daughter.

I was about to pick up the telephone to call to check on them, when it rang. Relief allowed my shoulders to relax; sure it would be Jim or Diane, telling me they were home.

It was Jim, but it wasn't good news, "Mom? I think something's wrong with Diane. I don't know what to do, Mom. I'm worried."

My body broke out in a cold sweat, and it felt as if my head was going to explode. My heart beat so fast, I thought it would crush my ribs.

"What is it, Jim? What's wrong? Where is she? Where's Diane?"

Fear caused his voice to tremble, "She's right here, Mom, lying on the bed. She's crying. She said she's hurting real bad."

Fighting to remain calm, I spoke in even tones, "Let me talk to her, Jim."

Jim gave her the phone, and I could hear frantic breathing that accompanies extreme pain.

"Mom? Something's wrong. Oh, Mom, I'm hurting so bad."

My mother's heart was being squeezed by a cruel fist. My daughter, my first-born, was in trouble, and she was almost a thousand miles away. With all my being, I wanted to hold her in my arms and make it better, just as I had when she was a little girl.

But Diane didn't need to hear the hysteria I felt, she needed a voice of calm reason.

"Where are you hurting, Diane?"

A soft moan escaped her lips, though I could tell she tried to suppress it.

"All over, Mom. I'm hurting everywhere."

"Sweetheart, I know you're hurting, but can you be a little more specific?"

She spoke through tightly clenched teeth; "It's my back, my lower stomach, and my legs."

Warning bells clanged in my spinning head, "When did all this start, honey?"

Her words caused me to draw in a sharp breath, "I think it may have started before I left your house. The longer we were on the road, the worse it got. Jim had to start driving before we got out of Oklahoma. By the time we got to Arkansas, I was rolling in the seat. We stopped at a rest area and I got out and walked around for a long time. It was the only thing I could think of the help the pain in my back. That's when my stomach and legs started hurting worse."

I covered the mouthpiece of the phone and began taking deep breaths.

It can't be! She's only twenty-seven weeks pregnant. Please, God, don't let her be in labor!

Her voice rose, "Mom?"

"Yes, baby, I'm still here."

When Diane spoke, I again heard the voice of the little girl I had kissed to make scraped knees feel better, "Mom? What should I do?"

Forcing a cheerfulness I didn't feel into my voice, "Well, honey, it may not be anything. It just may be that the trip was hard on you. Maybe you just need to rest. But, I really think you should call the doctor right away. He'll probably want to see you, so get Jim's mom to watch Christopher."

Her question was spoken in a soft tone, "I'm in trouble, aren't I, Mom?"

Not wanting to scare her, I said, "Honey, it might not be anything. Just promise me, though, that you'll call the doctor. Okay? Promise?"

"Oh, I promise, Mom. I'm hurting so much I couldn't put it off, even if I wanted to."

"Okay, honey. Let me speak to Jim, okay? I love you Diane."

"I love you, too, Mom. I wish you were here. I'm so scared."

I squeezed my eyes tightly; feeling the hot tears slip down my face. Jim answered, "Mom? What should we do?"

"Jim, first of all, you have to stay calm. She's going to need you, now maybe more than ever. Call the doctor—NOW."

I was so proud of Jim when I heard the forced bravery in his tone, "Okay. I'll call the doctor right away."

"Listen to me, Jim. Don't let Diane know what I'm saying, but I'm afraid she's in labor. She's got to get to the hospital, Jim!"

The terror almost, but not quite, slipped back into his voice, "You know, Mom, I think I'll just go ahead and take Diane to the emergency room. They can get the doctor to come in and check her out."

I knew he said that for Diane's benefit, since she was hanging on to his every word.

"Yes, honey. Take her to the hospital. And Jim? Hurry!"

Without another word, Jim hung up the phone. That was the beginning of the longest night of my life.

I didn't hear from either of them for several hours, and I paced the floor until my own back was aching. I wanted to call someone, anyone, to find out what was happening, but didn't know whom to contact.

I called Jim's mother, but there was no answer. I called his grandmother, but she wasn't home, either. I stepped away from the telephone, willing it to ring.

Three hours later, the phone finally rang. I jerked it up before it finished the first ring. It was Brenda, Jim's mother.

"Gloria? I wanted to call you and tell you what's going on. I know you're a nervous wreck, worrying about Diane."

"Brenda! What is it? What's going on? God, I've been scared to death!"

Regret filled her voice, "Gloria, it's not good. Jim took Diane to the emergency room and they called in her obstetrician. Dr. Decker told us Diane's in advanced labor."

I could feel the moan coming from the pit of my stomach, "Oh God, no! How is she? How're the babies?" Brenda began to cry, causing my terror to escalate, "She's weak, Gloria. Diane's so tired, and she's just begun the fight. They're worried about her. The babies?

Dr. Decker doesn't think they're going to make it. He said they're too small, and that twenty-seven weeks is too early, especially with twins. He's tried to prepare Diane and Jim. Jim is scared, but all he wants is for his wife to live. Diane was practically screaming at the doctor."

I could barely speak, "Screaming? From pain?"

Softly, "No, for the babies. Diane told the doctor to save the twins, no matter what. She said it doesn't matter if she makes it or not, just save the babies."

I no longer held back the tears, "No! Oh, no! Brenda, I can't lose her! I just can't. I want the twins to live, too. But if it's a choice between Diane or the babies, God help me, I would rather have my daughter."

Brenda's voice was filled with compassion, "I know, Gloria. I feel the same way. It would break my heart to lose the twins, but it would be worse to lose Diane."

"What are they going to do? Are they going to do surgery?"

"Yes, but..."

Fright made me impatient, "Yes, but what?"

Brenda hesitated for only a second that seemed an hour; "They've called in Life Flight. Diane's condition is so bad they're going to have to fly her to Knoxville. Dr. Decker said none of them have a chance of making it at our hospital here. I'm on my way to State Park, now. That's the closest open area that's large enough to land a helicopter. They said the 'copter should be here in twenty minutes. I only stopped at a pay phone long enough to call you. I know you're scared."

I was sobbing, and I'm sure Brenda had trouble understanding me, "Brenda, tell Diane you called me. You tell her that she promised me she'd take care of herself! Tell her I love her, and I'm begging God to watch over her. Please tell her, Brenda. Oh Lord, take care of my baby!"

Brenda was crying, "I'll tell her, Gloria. We're all praying for her and the babies. One of us will call you as soon as we get to Knoxville."

The minute I hung up the phone, I ran to the bathroom and was very sick. When it was over, I fell in the floor and cried. I talked to God, praying, bartering, promising.

I was so far away! I wanted to fly to Diane's side, but couldn't afford to. I wanted to jump in the car, but I also wanted to stay by the phone, just in case they called.

Another two hours passed with no word from anyone in Tennessee. I knew everyone there was petrified and were walking the floors just like me. But couldn't they at least call me? Just for a couple of minutes. Just to tell me my daughter was still alive. Surely that wasn't too much to ask.

My experience as a health care worker was just extensive enough to scare me to death about my own child's situation. Having been in the field for years, I knew how bad it must be in that helicopter. I walked outside, carrying the cordless telephone with me. I paced the front yard, my whole body feeling alive with insects. I scratched at my face, arms, and legs until I saw blood beneath my fingernails.

At last, at last, the phone rang!

It was Jim, "Mom. We're at the hospital."

"How is she, Jim? How is my baby girl?"

"They're taking her into surgery now. They're moving so fast, and using words I don't understand, and they don't seem to have time to explain anything to me. All I know is that Diane's not doing so well."

I knew he was trying to be brave for me, as well as himself, by sparing me the worst. But I wanted to reach into the phone and hit him!

"Jim, for God's sake, tell me! I'm so far away from her, and I can't be there to find out, so you have to be honest. Please!"

Jim began to cry, a sound that made my heart freeze, "They almost lost her, Mom. In the helicopter, Diane's heart stopped once. She's critical, but they hope to get her more stable."

I was having a great deal of trouble breathing, "What about the twins, Jim? How are the babies?"

Jim was quiet, almost as if he was afraid to say the words aloud, "It's bad, Mom. They've lost one of the heartbeats, and they're afraid one of the twins is gone. They're rushing Diane in for an emergency Cesarean, hoping they can save the other one. Mom, this is killing me!"

My heart went out to him; yet, at the same time I was in a fit of rage. Foolishly, I somehow blamed him. I was thinking if my daughter died, he had killed her. But that was insane, and I knew how wrong I was. I just couldn't help it.

But Jim didn't need, or deserve, recriminations, "Oh, Jim, I know you're scared. We're all scared. But Diane needs you now, and you can't let her down. You've got to be strong for her."

I could hear him sniffing, "I will, Mom. I'm going to go to surgery with her. I don't know how long this is gonna take, but I'll call you when it's over."

"Yes! I don't care what time it is, call me. Call me collect. Just call me! I won't be going to sleep tonight. Not unless I know Diane is alright."

"Bye, Mom. They said we're ready to go to OR."

"I love you, Jim. Be strong for your wife. Kiss her, and tell her I love her."

"I will, Mom."

The empty dial tone sounded grim.

Diane was in surgery for two hours. There were several close calls throughout the ordeal.

Diane had, in fact, gone into full labor, but the twins could never have made it through a normal delivery. The surgery was fast and frantic, and they were fighting for three lives, trying to rescue at least one of the twins from death.

The twins were a boy and a girl. It was the girl's heartbeat that the doctor could no longer detect. She was already in the birth canal, and in serious trouble. The doctor had to work her tiny head free, just to bring her into the world. The operating room staff worked with her until they were rewarded with a heartbeat. She was the first twin.

The baby boy, though having a heart beat, was even weaker than his sister. He was unresponsive, as if he was too small, and tired, to have the will to live.

The team of specialists in the room worked furiously with the miniature twins. Dr. Decker worked quickly to stabilize Diane, to enhance her chance for survival.

The twins were intubated and placed on ventilators. They were rushed to Neonatal Intensive Care immediately. The pediatrician was brutally honest and told Jim he doubted they lived.

Diane was taken to a room, and sedated heavily for pain. The staff watched her closely throughout the long night.

Jim called to tell me the surgery was over, but all three of them were still critical. I cried and thanked him for telling me the truth.

The next morning, Diane's medical status was upgraded to satisfactory condition. I thanked God, out loud, many times that day.

The twins weren't as fortunate. They couldn't breathe on their own, and their tiny hearts would stop beating at any given moment. The nurses would flip the bottom of their feet to start them breathing, or pick them up to work with them.

The twins needed so many medications, and they had to be given through an IV. Their veins were too small to find, so the doctors had to do what is called a "cut away", where the leg, itself, is cut open to reveal a vein that could support an IV needle. There were even needles in their heads.

Baby boy Adams weighed one pound, four ounces. Baby girl Adams weighed one pound even. Two very small human beings, fighting as hard as their little bodies would let them.

As soon as the doctor felt Diane was strong enough, he told her she could visit her twins in NICU. But, my daughter who loved children, my "Mother Earth", couldn't do it!

Jim and the rest of the staff tried, for days, to take her to see the twins. Diane didn't want to see them. Jim had even taken pictures of them, and brought them to her room. She had visions in her mind of a double funeral, with two tiny caskets covered in flowers. She thought if she never saw them, she could handle it better when they died.

The twins were valiant little fighters. Through the tube feedings, slowing or cessation of heartbeats, through all the needles covering their bodies, they fought. But the prognosis still looked bleak.

When the babies were four days old, Diane forced herself to go to them.

The nurse wheeled her down to NICU, and after showing her how to "scrub-up", put on a sterile gown, cap, and gloves, took Diane in to see her children for the first time.

Diane later told me she thought she would stop breathing the first time she saw her twins. It must have been the most horrible nightmare of a mother's life, seeing your children connected to all the machines and wires.

The NICU nurses took each one out of the incubator, and placed them in Diane's arms. She cried as she gazed at the two tiny creations she may never take home, and that, most likely, she would bury.

Now that she was there, time with her twins was a precious commodity. She sobbed when the nurses took them away from her to place them back in their incubators. She kissed each miniature face, and promised to come back as soon as they would let her.

As she was being wheeled back to her own room, Diane said, "They can't die! Not now! I love them, and I won't let them go."

Diane was released to go home in a week, but she begged to stay with her children. The doctor was adamant, telling her she needed to build her strength, and be with Christopher. She left the hospital with a broken heart.

Christopher was ecstatic to have Mommy back. It took several days to make him understand he couldn't jump up and down on Mommy, no matter how happy he was to see her.

Diane cared for Christopher, and prayed for the twins. Each day she and Jim made the seventy-mile round trip to visit their babies. Each day they thought would be the last time they saw them alive.

Every small improvement was a milestone for the twins. The oxygen on the ventilators was decreased in minute, careful increments. Each decreased dosage of medicine through the IV was a cause of celebration.

Al and I drove to Tennessee to see my twin grandchildren just before Christmas. I thought it might be the only time I would get to be with them.

We scrubbed up to visit the babies in NICU. When I saw all the tubes connected to their little bodies, I had to restrain myself to keep from crying. Even though I worked with similar machines, these were my grandchildren I was seeing.

The boy was too critical to be removed from his incubator. The girl was just a little stronger, so the nurse put her in my arms.

I held her, and talked to her, as if I'd never see her again, because I was certain I wouldn't. While I still held her, a nurse ran to me and pulled the baby from my arms. I was startled, and asked what was wrong.

"Didn't you hear the monitor alarming? She had stopped breathing, and I had to remind her to take a breath."

I was scared, and felt guilty. My own granddaughter had stopped breathing and I didn't even know it! All my medical training seemed to have vanished when it came to these two babies of my own flesh and blood.

Christmas that year was a sad one for all of us. I hated to go back home, wanting to stay near the babies, and Diane, as long as possible. But, no matter what happens, bills and life go on. Al and I had to get back to work.

I called for updates every day. Some days I even heard good news.

The improvement in the twins was a very long, very hard, uphill battle. So many prayers were said for the twins that God must have decided they should remain with their family.

For a week, Diane and Jim were given a room near the twins, and taught infant CPR. Both of the babies spent most of the time with their parents, wearing the apnea monitors they would keep for another year.

The week of the twin's original due date, Baby Girl Adams went home. Her name was Amber, and Christopher was very excited to meet her.

Baby Boy Adams, also known as Jonathan, stayed in the hospital for almost another month. Christopher was amazed when yet another baby was brought into the house.

In fact, for a few months, each time Diane and Jim left the house, Christopher thought they were going to bring home another baby.

There have been good times, and bad, for Amber and Jonathan. They were so far behind their chronological age; it took them quite some time to catch up.

They had trouble keeping food down for many months. The apnea alarm monitors went off several times, every night. With the first *bleep* of the alarm, Diane and Jim both jumped up and ran to the twins, even before they were completely awake. When I would visit, I realized how frightening it must be for these young parents with the fragile babies.

Then there was the time when a pediatrician thought they had cerebral palsy. Another bleak period in the twins' history. But, thankfully, it turned out to be a false alarm.

It took them a little longer to sit up, walk, and talk, than many other babies, but they did it!

Amber and Jonathan will soon be ten years old. Amber has won certificates and prizes for being such a good student, and helping her classmates. She's had her picture in the newspaper more than once.

Jonathan is our family's best ballplayer. He played T-ball, then graduated to baseball. He has an entire shelf of trophies to prove it.

We've had yet one more miracle in our family. Her name is Stephanie, and she was born, without any medical fanfare, two years after the twins.

All of Diane's children are precious, just as she is, and I can't imagine life without these beautiful people.

So each time I see Amber's smiling face in the newspaper or I watch Jonathan bring home another trophy, I think, "And these were the babies they said wouldn't live."

I believe God knew we needed them, and would treasure them as much as He does.

In the Darkest Hour

The night shift in ER can be as quiet as a mausoleum, or pervaded with agonizing, cursing, pathetic cries from the depths of Hell. We, the harried staff trying to man a trauma unit with a too-short staff, know this well. You'll usually find us rushing around, trying to be in several places at once. We're either overwhelmed with patients or withering from boredom. But more often, there is so much trauma, illness, and death, it all seems to blur together.

Some patients pass through so quickly and their injuries are not severe enough to linger in your mind. There are, however, a few that leave such an impact on your psyche, the memory of them will remain there for the rest of your life. Some we remember with humor, some with sadness, and some with a shiver that races down our spines. I've had a few of those, but only one that truly terrified me.

It was a Saturday night and uncharacteristically quiet. We usually called the weekend in the emergency department as our "Gun and Knife Show". It seemed as if most of our patients had been involved in a drunken or drug-induced argument and came out on the wrong end of the fight.

One of the nurses was telling me about yet another new guy she'd met and laughed when I unintentionally yawned. We were only an hour into the shift; just before midnight, when we got the call from EMSA that they were bringing in a double attempted suicide. Since they said, "attempted" we at least knew the patients were still alive. Also, since it was more than one, we assumed it was some sort of suicide pact. With suppositions running through our minds, we raised our eyebrows at each other and began preparing for their arrival. I could hear the ambulance siren wailing even as the paramedic was still phoning in his report. We helped each other tie our surgical gowns closed and threw rubber gloves to each other. I had just pulled my stethoscope from my pocket when I heard the screaming siren wind down outside. Little did any of us know this was to be the experience of a lifetime.

The doors crashed open at 12:05 AM, and I could feel the blood start hammering through my veins. It doesn't matter how many times you go through it, an emergency sends adrenaline rushing through your body. You function as a professional, but you never become immune to the urgency. This is the time when ER resembles a battle zone, with frantic movements, yelled instructions, and people bouncing off each other in their haste to save lives. To an observer, it must look like pandemonium, but nothing could be further from the truth.

Another thing the observer may think is that medical personnel are cold, unfeeling people. Another misconception. We have, unfortunately, had to disassociate ourselves from the pain and suffering of the patient in our care, only so we can retain our own sanity. To become completely immersed in every case would cause us to lose our effectiveness. That, however, does *not* mean that we don't feel, nor have any compassion. Most of us think of our own loved ones in a similar situation or "But for the grace of God, there go I". I truly believe that lay people would be amazed at how often we cry, scream, or curse at life's injustices, and the cruelty inflicted on the human body. Even when the pain is self-inflicted, as with this case, we work just as hard, just as quickly, to save that life.

The paramedics ran down the hallway with our two newest patients, a man and a woman. They were placed in separate rooms, with each being surrounded by a rather large group of people, desperately trying to save the life that they, in some horrible desperation, had tried to extinguish.

Being a respiratory therapist, I was running back and forth between the two patients, accessing the situation, until I found the greatest need for my services was with the female. I was to regret that turn of events, believe me. I felt it was going to be a long night. If only I'd known how correct I was in that assumption.

Both of them were very attractive people. The man was large, dark hair, dark eyes, and had an athletic physique, as if he worked out often. It was apparent he was tanned beneath the pallor of his self-induced coma. A wide, white circle remained after we removed his wedding ring.

The woman was so tiny! She looked to be just above five feet tall, with the lithe body of a woman that took care of herself. She had long, natural blonde hair, and green eyes. Lying there, she resembled a doll, or a princess asleep. Even during the busy hustle to save them, I had time to wonder why two such people would want to die.

Tables covered with different instruments and chemicals were next to each of them. The methods we used would be the same for both patients. Long tubing was inserted into the nostril so we could pump in charcoal to combat the affects of the drug overdose each of them had taken. It was later discovered they had divided a bottle of prescription sleeping pills between them. We intubated them with endotracheal tubes to keep their airways open and then attached them to ventilators. We suctioned them, pumped IV solutions into their bodies, and began running numerous tests. Most of us compressed our lips in silent outrage and despair that two healthy people would want to die this way. When we have patients that fight for their next breath just to say alive a few minutes more, it seems a disgrace that healthy people would try to kill a healthy body.

The biggest difference between the two patients was their reaction to us, and what was being done to them, once they began to regain consciousness.

The man, whom I found out was named Marc, was compliant and still. It seemed he was angrily quiet, as if he was resigned to the fact that we were going to save his life, whether he liked it or not. He lay there, watching all that went on around him, and never moved. He adopted the attitude that he was alone, that we weren't there, and he stared at the ceiling.

Our pretty blonde princess, named Sharon, was a study in hysteria.

From the moment she awoke, she became like a woman possessed. She opened her eyes, sat up on the gurney, and began to pull needles from her body. Before we could grab her determined hands, she had ripped out the tube that had regulated her breathing.

The moment her airway was clear, Sharon began to scream. Not in anger, not in relief, but in terror. Sharon wasn't upset that she was still alive, as was Marc. She was horrified by what she obviously thought she saw when she looked at us, the hospital staff valiantly trying to save her life.

As I was the respiratory therapist in attendance, it was my job to use the ambu bag to "breathe" the patient until we could reinsert the tube for the ventilator. It was quite evident she wasn't going to be able to breathe on her own for very long, and that she was using all her lung capacity and energy to scream. We were going to have to hold her down to intubate her again.

It took four nurses and two doctors to hold down this tiny, ferocious woman so that leather restraining straps could be put on her arms and legs. I was busy trying to hold her head still and keep the ambu bag over her face to give her oxygen. It was from this close proximity that I had an excellent viewpoint of Sharon's facial expressions, and hear her words. It was a look I'll never forget; though I've tried to, many times. It was a look of pure, unadulterated terror.

Sharon's blood-shot eyes were opened wide, at times seeming to roll back into her head, so great was her fear. Saliva dripped from her blue lips, pulled back against her teeth. Spittle flew as she screamed into my face, and she thrashed around, slamming her head against the hard metal of the gurney, time and time again. Though some of the words were screamed with such intense fear, I managed to understand most of them. God help me, I wish I hadn't.

"Leave me alone! You hear me? Stop it! No, God please, no! Get away from me! God help me, please! I'm so scared, God. Please, please, please help me! Please God! Please! See 'em, God? See all of 'em standing here? Ooh, God, please help me! It's the demons, God. Demons from Hell! God please, don't let 'em take me! Please, sweet Jesus in Heaven, save me!"

I stood there, holding her head, administering life-sustaining oxygen, yet I could still hear her muffled screams of terror echoing through the rubber of the ambu bag.

Staff members that work the emergency room have seen some amazing things. I have been known to say, when asked if I liked my job, "It is, at the same time, the most wonderful and the most horrible job in the world." This night was to be one of the worst.

Sharon continued to fight like an injured, raging tiger. Even though held down by leather restraints, she managed to bruise most of us that were working closest to her body. She kicked us, and repeatedly tried to bite our hands and arms. She managed to tear into the rubber of the ambu mask and I quickly ripped open the package of another one. Her teeth slammed against each other as she tried to move her head enough to bite me. It is surprising how badly a patient can hurt a health care worker, even when they're supposedly immobile.

Just before 3 AM, Sharon somehow, amazingly, escaped one of the leather straps holding her arm. The first thing she pulled was the airway tube, and her terrified screams again filled the emergency department. Staff members came from all directions and ran into the room.

Foam covered her lips and her eyes were moving wildly about the room. "God! Please! Sweet Jesus in all your mercy...! Lord, please help me! They're killing me! Get away from me! Please, for the love of God, get away from me! Noooooooooo, please God, no! Demons! Demons from Hell, trying to kill me, God! Pleeeeeeeease! Jeeeeeeee Sus!"

Sharon's small arm was being held by one of the nurses, and the doctor was attempting to buckle the leather strap back into place. She pulled free and hit the doctor in the face, knocking his glasses to the floor, and above the screams, I could hear the lens to shatter on impact.

Sharon then drew her hand back once more, slamming her fist into the nurse's face, breaking her nose in a shower of blood. The nurse grabbed a towel and placed it over her nose, which covered her look of incredulous surprise.

I was trying to hold the ambu bag, once more, on Sharon's face, as she was thrashing her head from side to side. At the same time, I was quickly preparing the sterile tray of intubation supplies for the doctor working frantically by my side.

During all this, Sharon continued to scream at us, the demons from Hell, and beg God to help her. The look on her face, as she stared into mine, is something that is carved indelibly on my life's worst memories. Even now, I still have nightmares with Sharon in the leading role.

Just as we managed to buckle her arm again, and as we were trying to reinsert the airway tube to help her tiring lungs, Sharon suddenly changed her demeanor. Even her tone of voice was now different. Where she had been screaming in terror, she now hissed in a horrible, somehow *demented* manner. She stared into my face and hissed, "I'll get you! As God is my witness, I'll kill you!"

Shaken, but determined to not show it, I continued my duty. Just as the tube was placed against her lips, she cackled as she hissed into my face, "I'll see you in Hell!"

I have never, in all my years of medical experience, been so relieved to have a patient intubated so they could no longer speak. After the ventilator was once more stabilizing her breath rate, I leaned against a cabinet and heaved a sigh of relief.

Another respiratory therapist came into the exam room to check on our progress with Sharon. It was then that we learned, at least for the moment, Marc was in stable condition, and had been transported to Intensive Care. It was only a small victory, and could be a short-lived one, but we would take any we could get. We were so emotionally drained already; we needed any good news someone could give us.

It would have been helpful if we could have strongly medicated our princess. But because Sharon had taken an overdose of narcotics, the doctors were very limited in what medicine they could inject into the IV tubing. We wanted to save her, and knew that a strong sedative may kill her. She was given low dosages to calm her, which allowed us to conduct our various tests, and hopefully keep her alive.

For the next long seven hours, Sharon lapsed in and out of

consciousness. Each time she opened her eyes, she had that terrified look of unmitigated horror as she watched us, and tried to wrestle free of her restraints. Her arms and legs became chaffed from her straining against the leather.

It was during one of Sharon's restful periods that I stepped out to the nurse's station, leaving her side for the first time in five hours. Two nurses were still with her, watching monitors and writing notes. All I wanted was a fast cup of coffee and a deep breath of air. I thought I might find a quiet corner where I could stand and sip my coffee, but it wasn't meant to be.

In the middle of the room there was a large group of people. They were standing near the nurse's station, yelling, crying, and gesturing wildly. This may sound odd to you but it's a common occurrence in any ER. As I stepped closer, I began to make out words that were being tossed around in heated anger.

A tall, burly man who looked to be in his thirties was yelling at a pretty woman, whose head was bent as she sobbed,

"This is all Marc's fault! He did this! If he does live, I'm going to kill him! Sharon was just fine till he came along. If I lose her, I swear to God…"

The weeping woman pushed her hair away from her face to dab a tissue against the flood of tears. In a flash I understood what I was hearing. The weeping woman was Marc's wife, and the violently angry man was Sharon's husband!

I turned my head from the scene as I thought, *Oh no, they were married—to other people! How many lives this reckless act has affected!*

My attention was drawn back to the agitated group when I heard Marc's wife speak in a voice barely above a whisper, "I don't understand. I love him! In fact, I love Marc so much that I would've given him a divorce to be with Sharon before I would have him kill himself. Why didn't he just tell me? I would've let him go." My heart ached for this sad, defeated lady, waiting to hear if her husband would live or die.

Sharon's husband became so irate at those words security had to be called to escort him from the ER. He was ushered outside the automatic sliding doors and counseled until he was calm enough to come back into the hospital. Once inside, he was taken to another waiting room, and told a doctor would be in to speak with him soon.

Marc's wife was led from the ER to the elevators down the hall. One of our nurses put her arm around the distraught woman and escorted her to Intensive Care to be with her husband.

The span between the tic and the next tock of the clock seemed to last for hours. Just at 6 AM, Sharon came out of her restless slumber to take one last stand against the demons that surrounded her.

It appeared that Sharon was much more alert at this point, and had adapted a stealthy plan to break free and escape. We were again in the room with her, going over her chart lying on the counter next to the gurney. It was only when the alarms went off that we knew what she had been doing.

We had been watching her carefully, knowing she was bent on self-destruction. Each time we looked at her, Sharon's eyes would be closed, and her breathing was the same regular pattern the ventilator was programmed to supply.

Since she was restrained so well that she could no longer pull her arms free, Sharon had devised a plan to twist her head, as far as humanly possible, to pull the airway tube from her throat, and her starving lungs.

It must have been with superhuman effort that Sharon managed to sit up, pulling the tube from her lips. The ventilator alarms filled the small exam room, and we turned as Sharon spat at us.

"Demons from Hell! Let me go! Cut me loose! You're not taking me to Hell with you! God, help me!"

Sharon's eyes were again rolling wildly, and blood covered her white lips. I grabbed the ambu bag, ready to repeat the performances of earlier that morning. It was at this moment that Sharon's heart ceased to beat.

Sharon had gone into full cardiac arrest. What had been an effort to keep her calm and flush the poison from her system now turned into a "Code Blue".

As I pressed the rubber mask of the ambu bag to her now purple face, I could hear the call over the PA system, alerting all personnel that another life was slipping away from us.

The room filled with more people than we needed. The doctor had to decide who he needed and ask the others to wait outside the small room. Those of us left almost wished we had been asked to leave.

For the next hour, we fought with death, and Sharon's demons.

We worked until she regained consciousness once again, and listened to her screams of terror and appeals to God.

The doctor reintubated her, and the ventilator did the best it had been programmed to do, to keep her breathing.

Sharon was now attached to so many machines and wires; she barely resembled a human, more like some type of grotesque robot.

But all the wires, all the machines in the world can't save everyone. When the cardiac monitor displayed a flat line for the fifth time that last hour, we tried even harder to coax her heart back into a rhythm. But, this time, Sharon's tired heart refused, and we lost her. Just after 7 AM, Sharon died.

Usually a person's face will relax in death, seeming to be relieved of the burden of the pain. Sharon's face wasn't relaxed. It was twisted into the same grimace of terror I had seen for most of the last seven hours.

After we had turned off all the alarming monitors, after we had removed tubes and wires from the small body, I stood beside the young woman I had helped fight to save.

I lay my hand upon hers, and closed my eyes against my tears. As I did so, I prayed for Sharon, and hoped she'd had time to find peace with her God before she was taken away.

The prognosis for Marc was a happy one. The difference in his and Sharon's body size had been the only thing that had saved him. Because he was large, his body had been able to fend off the narcotic better than Sharon's small one had. I prayed for Marc and his wife many times, hoping they were able to save their troubled marriage.

Several weeks after the suicide attempt, Marc came to visit us, to thank us for working so hard to save him. As he walked in, I smiled to see his lovely wife was with him, and they were holding hands. He told us that they had been going to counseling and it helped them to sort out the bitter, hurtful feelings his actions have caused.

As I write this, I remember a few things I heard from other staff members that night. Most people think that, while health care workers may believe in God, they push it aside while they practice medicine. It is those people that I wish could have heard us during those long seven hours.

One of our nurses, during one of the screaming bouts, stroked Sharon's hair, trying to calm her. As she did, she prayed, beneath her breath, for the tortured soul before her. In fact, most of us prayed for Sharon that night.

So you see, yes, we deal in medical science. We practice in the field that we love. Yet we are sensitive, caring, saddened individuals. Yes, most of us believe in God. Most of us talk to Him every time we walk into whichever hospital we work.

I know, without a doubt, that all of us were talking to God to save Sharon. I would like to believe He did.

Not My Child

"We're sorry, Mrs. Jobe, but the news about your baby isn't good."

My eyes grew wide, and I had lost the power of speech. I hadn't, though, lost the ability to think. My mind was racing, imagining the worst. One of the unfortunate aspects of being in the medical field is knowing just enough about medicine to be terrified when it comes to one of your own. Finally, I was able to ask the dreaded question.

"What's wrong with her? Is she...? Is she dead?"

The doctor, with his nurse at his side, was quick to tell me my baby was very much alive, but she had some serious medical problems.

"Mrs. Jobe, the baby has turned very yellow, and we believe she is jaundiced. While that in itself is usually nothing too serious, she has some other problems that we are just now finding. We can put her under a sun lamp and that will most likely get rid of the jaundice. However..."

My mouth was dry and my pulse was racing.

"Please doctor, will you just tell me? You're scaring me by dragging this out. I'm a respiratory practitioner and I can take it. Just get it over with, please."

The doctor took my hand, a gesture meant to calm me, only made me more nervous.

"I have called in a pediatric specialist, Mrs. Jobe. While examining the baby, I distinctly heard a heart murmur. Again, not necessarily a major problem. Many children are born with this and they grow out of it. But your baby seems to be very weak, and there is a bluish tinge around her eyes, lips, and fingernails."

It felt as if someone were squeezing the breath from my lungs. What was he taking so long to try to tell me?

"I'm pretty sure where all this is leading, but I want to be certain. What exactly does all this mean, Doctor?"

"I'm not a cardiologist, Mrs. Jobe, but I believe the baby may have a serious congenital heart defect. I'm sorry, but I can't tell you anymore just now. The specialist should be here this afternoon and he will be conducting tests on her. With your permission, of course."

"Of course! Anything. Everything. Whatever it takes, just make her well. I'll do whatever you want, just take care of my baby."

The doctor rose from the side of my bed, patted my hand, and left my room with his nurse behind him.

I lay there staring at the ceiling, praying for God to heal my daughter. She was only four hours old and in trouble.

The day seemed to go on for weeks. No one else came in to speak with me about my daughter and all I had to do was lie there, worrying.

That afternoon was the first time I got to actually hold her. When she was put in my arms, her name became Linda, Latin for beautiful.

I cuddled her close, kissed her sweet face, and cried. Her small lips that should have been rosebud pink were, indeed, quite blue. The veins in her eyelids were in sharp contrast to her pale skin. She cried very little, but when she did, it sounded weak, defeated.

I unwrapped her pink blanket and, like all mothers, I counted her fingers and toes. They were also blue, but at least they were all accounted for. Not accounted for was the way I could see her little chest moving, as if I could actually see her heart beating.

Before I could finish trying to get her to eat, a nurse came in to take her away. I started to cry again and asked her to let me keep her for a few minutes more. The nurse gently explained that the pediatric cardiologist was there and wanted to examine the baby. Even more afraid now that she had told me, I kissed my baby's soft cheek and let the nurse take her from my arms.

Again, the hours dragged past. How long could it possibly take to run those tests? I was anxious to hear what they had found out, but terrified at the same time. Around five o'clock, the delivering doctor came back, and with him was the cardiologist. I could tell by their faces that it wasn't good news. I'd seen similar expressions as physicians told family members news that would devastate their lives. I listened with my ears, but my mother's heart rebelled at the news.

"Mrs. Jobe, this is Dr. Campbell, the specialist I spoke with you about. He has examined the baby…"

No matter what they were going to tell me, I felt it absolutely necessary they should refer to her by her name, not just by "the baby".

"Linda. Her name is Linda."

Dr. Campbell took my hand, much the same way the other doctor had earlier in the day. It was less reassuring now than before.

"Mrs. Jobe, I'm sorry, but it's not good news. As Dr. Price told you, there is a distinct heart murmur. Yes, most children can, and do, outgrow those, but Linda won't. This problem is gravely compounded by the fact that her heart is terribly enlarged. In fact, her heart is the size of two normal hearts, resting side by side. Linda's heart completely covers her entire chest."

I buried my face in my pillow, willing him to be quiet, and sobbing until I was getting sick.

No, no, God no! Not my baby!

I couldn't escape the cardiologist's voice, no matter how hard I tried.

"Mrs. Jobe, please listen to me. I am going to need you to help me with her problems. Linda is going to need you, very badly. She can't do this without you."

Do what without me? They had just given my baby a death sentence. What could I do to help her? Die?

"Mrs. Jobe, Linda is a very weak little girl. Her chances for survival aren't good. I would estimate her odds at 75 to 25 per cent – *against* her."

My world shattered. It *was* a death sentence.

"You must listen to me! She still has that 25 per cent chance. You have to help her make the most of it. If Linda lives to be four years old, she will have to have open-heart surgery. We don't dare attempt to do it any sooner; she's just too weak. If she makes it that long, we will have to build her up for surgery. I don't mean to sound callous or unfeeling, dear. It's just that you have to understand the magnitude of this situation."

My hopes lifted. If he was talking about surgery, surely he felt she just might make it. Just a chance, but that was all I asked for.

"Yes! I told Dr. Price 'Anything. I'll do anything to save her. Just tell me what to do.'"

Dr. Campbell patted my hand before he began the list of things I would need to follow.

"You are going to have to watch her very carefully. I know that everyone is going to tell you it's good for a baby to cry. And in most cases it is, but not this time. I don't mean for you to run to her bed each time she whimpers, but don't let her cry for a long period of time. It will only wear out her already-tired heart. Watch for signs of difficulty in breathing. If she appears to stop breathing, pick her up immediately and massage her back, stomach, anything to make her breathe again. I'm going to prescribe vitamins to help build her strength. Make sure she gets them twice a day. I want you to have her on a special formula, and I'll write down the name of it for you. I'll be making arrangements for you and your husband to learn infant CPR before you take her home."

I had been staring at his face as he spoke, and my eyes once more filled with tears when he stopped speaking.

"That's it? Is this all the advice you have to give me? Nothing else?"

Dr. Campbell sighed, "Yes, Mrs. Jobe, one more thing. Watch her, take care of her and love her like each day is the last, then pray that it isn't."

I lay in the quickly approaching twilight, staring at the door they used to walk out on me. I thought of Jennifer, my fourteen month old waiting at home. Oh God, what was I going to do?

Linda was started on an intravenous medication, building her up so she could go home with me. Her condition did not improve, nor did it grow worse.

When my baby was five days old, I took her home. I was terrified, but I thanked God for letting me have her for one more day.

All the friends and relatives started making their rounds, visiting the new baby. They all said she was pretty, just like they always do. Everyone remembered to play with Jennifer so she didn't feel left out of all the attention.

Some of them had said Linda looked like she was sleepy all the time. She did because she was so weak. Her cry was like a wounded kitten. Her appetite was terrible, and I would sit for hours, coaxing her to eat. Many times I would manage to make her eat, only to have her vomit everything I had just gotten into her.

I fed her, bathed her, and gave her vitamins—everything I'd been told to do. Every day I had her, I prayed for one more. Just one more day, God, for another four years.

When Linda was two weeks old, she developed pneumonia. She was put back into the hospital, and I stayed with her day and night. She lay in her crib wearing nothing but a diaper, with a cold mist pouring into her bed. If I hadn't been trained in respiratory illnesses, I would have sworn that would have killed her. She pulled through and went home in three days. Jennifer was happy to have her baby sister back.

Before Linda was released this time, Dr. Campbell spoke with me. He once more cautioned me about her care. He then told me he wanted to see Linda on or near her first birthday, unless she needed him sooner. Again, although he was kind, I was left with the impression that there was little or no hope and all I could do was pray.

And I did. I prayed when I woke in the morning, I prayed as I fed her, and I prayed as I put her to bed at night.

I wasn't getting much sleep. I had put Linda's crib against the side of my bed, just so I could hear her breathe, or if she needed me. Several times I awakened because I didn't hear the rhythmic breathing I had grown used to. I would briskly rub her back, and she would start to breathe again.

Linda made it to her first birthday. She still wasn't walking or trying to talk in a baby's special language. At this point, she could barely sit up on her own. I made the appointment for the cardiologist to see my baby, for what I wishfully called her first annual check-up.

My hopes for a good report were dashed when Dr. Campbell handed Linda to me, after running more tests.

"The x-rays show no improvement, Mrs. Jobe. I'm sorry. Linda's condition is the same as when she was born. Graduate her to more solid food, and continue everything else you've been doing."

"Oh, I will, Doctor. You can count on me. Linda and I will see you in about a year to celebrate her second birthday."

"I hope so, Mrs. Jobe. I sure hope so."

When I got home, I held both my little girls in my arms and sang to them, careful to not let them know my heart was breaking.

Linda started walking when she was eighteen months old. It was a long, drawn-out ordeal because she was too weak to stand for very long. But she did it! She continued to look sleepy, even after a long nap. The veins in her eyelids stood out, and her lips never completely lost that slightly blue tint.

Linda's second birthday again found us at Dr. Campbell's clinic. The results were, again, the same. Same speech, same instructions.

Linda began to play more vigorously, imitating her older sister, and I was always afraid she would over-extend herself. It seemed, though, that there was a safety mechanism built into her little body. Whenever she played too much, she just took a nap. All in all, things were going fairly smoothly.

Two months before Linda's third birthday, she got a terrible cold, which rapidly turned into influenza. She was a very sick little girl when I took her to her pediatrician. He told me to give her baby aspirin.

"I'll try to make her take them, Doctor. She hates them and really fusses when I put on in her mouth. I've even tried dissolving one in a spoon, but she spits that out, too."

"Well, you *must* to make her take it, even if you have to force it on her. She needs the aspirin to get well, and she can't take being this sick for much longer. Take her home and make her take the aspirin."

When it came time to take the aspirin, Linda refused to take it, as always. I dissolved two in a spoon and she spit it out faster than I could get it all in her mouth. I told Larry, my husband, we had to make her take it, just as the doctor instructed me. I always followed doctor's orders.

I opened her mouth and put the aspirin in. Larry and I were trying to get her to swallow it when Linda seemed to choke. She started turning a deep blue, almost purple, and her mouth was sealed tightly. We couldn't get her mouth open, and couldn't get her to respond to us. Her back became stiff as a board, and she was losing consciousness. Larry and I began to pass her back and forth between us, frantically trying to save her.

Larry grabbed her and ran toward the front door. He later said he had no idea where he was going, he just had to get Linda out of the house. I ran ahead of him, also not knowing what he was doing, and opened the door. Larry ran outside with our baby.

It was snowing that night and was blistering cold. When the snow hit Linda's face, she gasped, and amazingly swallowed the aspirin. Then she immediately passed out.

We called an ambulance; sure she wouldn't make it until it arrived. They rushed her to the emergency room where they summoned Dr. Campbell. After conducting many tests, he told us Linda had had a mild heart attack. He said another one would kill her.

After spending several days in the hospital, Linda was released back into our care. I was more terrified than ever, certain I couldn't keep her alive much longer.

Linda's third birthday brought a feeling of accomplishment for me. She had lived three years longer than expected. One more year and we could try surgery. I was more hopeful than ever before.

The all-day examination at Dr. Campbell's clinic proved there was to be no promising words for Linda. Her heart was worse than when she was born due to the heart attack she had experienced.

"Mrs. Jobe, you've proven what strong power a mother's love can have. You've kept her alive much longer than I expected. One more year, Mrs. Jobe, and we can perform surgery. One more year."

The next year was one of many changes for Linda. Her older sister started kindergarten and Linda was jealous. She was so in love with the idea of going to school it was hard for me to explain to her why she couldn't go with her sister.

Linda would watch Jennifer when she wrote her letters on paper, and mimic the image on her own bedroom walls. I used a lot of cleanser for a few months.

Jennifer would bring one of her school friends home and Linda would become frustrated when she didn't have the stamina to keep up with their roughhousing.

At night, Jennifer would be jumping around the living room, full of five-year-old energy. Linda would just lie on the couch giggling at her sister's antics, yet she resented it.

I thought that if Linda couldn't yet attend regular school, she could still enjoy Sunday school. I started taking both girls to church every Sunday, and they both loved it. Linda lost all her resentment because she felt she was going to school, too.

I told many of the church members about Linda's condition and prognosis. I know that there were many times Linda was prayed for by the church members. I was present at some, and was told about many others. I was thankful; we needed all the help we could get.

Linda's fourth birthday was a celebration in every way imaginable. This frail, tiny, pale little girl had made it! I looked forward to the appointment with Dr. Campbell, sure that we could now make it through surgery.

Once more, I walked away, my spirit crushed.

"Linda has done fairly well, but I don't feel she is quite strong enough for surgery. Not yet. We need to build her body, build her strength. Let's increase the vitamins and start low-impact exercises for a while longer. Bring her back in six months and we'll see where we stand."

In church that next Sunday, I told my friends the sad news. Their answer was renewed prayers. I prayed, but I was quickly losing hope.

That August, we had a surprise come into our lives. My half-sister, whom I had never met, came to visit. We were all excited, but Linda was thrilled. She had just found out she had an aunt and three cousins she'd never met. She sat by the window, waiting for their car to pull into the driveway.

During the day, my sister and I got to know each other a little better. We discovered neither of us had ever been to our father's grave. It was decided that's what we should do the next day.

Early the next morning, we all met for breakfast. We were happy to at last visit our father's final resting-place. As neither one of us were from the area and didn't know the exact location, my sister found a relative to show us the way.

It was a rather somber occasion, but it seemed to bring some sort of closure to the empty spot I had been carrying in my heart. My father had died when I was four and I had no memories of him. Visiting him somehow helped the ache.

As all of us climbed back into my sister's station wagon, we were smiling through our tears. The kids climbed in the back, ready to make the long trip back home.

As we were backing, downhill, out of the gravel parking lot of the church, a terrible thing happened. I don't know exactly what it was that alerted us, but my sister pushed the brake to stop the car.

I looked to the back of the car and saw the door swinging open. At a time like that everything seems to move in slow motion. I remember thinking to myself, "There were five children back there, but now there's only four. One of them is gone, but which one?"

By the time I jumped from the car and ran to the back, I realized it was Linda. But when I got there, she was nowhere to be found. From underneath the car, I hear a whimper.

"Mommy? Please Mommy, get me out. My head hurts so bad. Please, Mommy."

I knelt in the rocks, and there was my baby, trapped beneath the car. She wasn't crying, just repeatedly asking me to get her out.

I tried to careful remove her, but her head was stuck. There was some type of hook on the underside of the car and it was wedged against her head. We didn't realize that at the time or things may have turned out differently.

My sister's husband jumped into the driver's seat and drove the car forward, pulling it off Linda. When he did so, the hook that had been pressing into her head tore her scalp open.

When I could at last reach her, I pulled Linda into my arms. She was dirty and already bruising. I noticed that her hair, which I had put up in ponytails, looked strange. One ponytail was high on her head, while the other one was brushing her shoulder. I just assumed it was pulled down while she was under the car.

Linda wasn't crying. She wasn't doing anything except staring at me.

"Mommy, am I okay? It sure was scary down there."

I brushed her face with my hands, this little person that was acting tough as nails. She was just shaken up. We all were. But again, Linda was alright.

My sister stood beside me, crying. I motioned for her to stop, and whispered she would scare Linda.

"Linda? Are you okay, honey? I'm so sorry, Sweetie."

Linda turned to her aunt with a smile, and began to tell her that everything was okay, she was fine. As soon as Linda turned her head I knew she was anything *but* fine.

The reason her ponytail was drooping was because Linda's scalp had been ripped open. Each time Linda's heart would beat, blood and small pieces of flesh were spraying anything near. The side of her dress was rapidly becoming saturated, and Linda didn't even seem to notice.

I've always wanted to be strong for my loved ones, especially my children. But I am almost ashamed to admit that, for a few seconds, I lost it. When I saw my little girl's skull exposed, and all the blood she was losing, I almost fell apart. I stared up at the sky and repeated what I had said just four short years ago.

"Oh God, no! Not my baby!"

"Mommy? What's the matter? Am I okay, Mommy?"

Hearing the rising panic in her voice, I regained my composure with lightning speed. No matter what happened, I knew my child needed me and the loving strength she had always counted on to be there.

"Yes, baby, yes. You're okay. Oh, I think you may have bumped your head pretty good. We'll just take you to the hospital and, you know, just let the doctor kind of check you out. How's that with you?"

Linda's eyes were round and large in her little face.

"You sure I'm okay, Mommy?"

"Oh sure. I think you may need a bandage or two, but you're just fine."

I wanted to pick up my daughter and run screaming down the hill, begging God, in all His mercy, to save her, just one more time. Instead, I calmly took her hand and led her back to the car. I got in, sat Linda on my lap, and told the others to get in the car with us.

We drove down the road, none of us knowing exactly where we were. Even the relative that had shown us the way was too upset to be of much use. The adults in the front seat began to cry, loudly. When they did, Linda looked at me as if to ask what was wrong with everyone?

I couldn't let Linda know how badly she was injured, but I had to tell the adults in the front to calm down. I began to spell out my message. I spelled to them that if she knew how bad it was, Linda would have another heart attack, and she would die. I spelled that they had to stop crying; they had to stop scaring Linda.

Complete silence descended, with the exception of a whimpering from behind me. It was Jennifer, crying over her sister, and very scared. At one point Jennifer leaned over the seat to whisper in my ear.

"Mommy? Sissy's gonna die, isn't she?"

Terrified myself, I regret I was almost angry with Jennifer for daring to even utter those words.

"No! Now stop saying that. Sit down and be a good girl for Mommy. We're taking Sissy to see the doctor and she's going to be just fine."

I kissed my older daughter's face to take the sting from my words.

We spotted a police car parked at a restaurant. I told my sister to pull over and ask him to take us to the hospital. I was careful to keep my tone of voice calm, determined Linda wouldn't know I was near hysteria.

The officer ran out of the restaurant, took one look at Linda in my arms, and jumped into his patrol car. He turned the lights and siren on, and began to escort us to the hospital.

Linda began to grow limp in my arms, and her eyes were closing. I knew I couldn't let her go to sleep; she may never wake up if she did.

"Linda. Wake up, honey. Come on, talk to me. Want to sing a song? Want to sing 'This Old Man'? Come on, Sweetie; don't go to sleep on me. Okay?"

Linda's head was still wobbly on her neck but she managed to get her eyes open. When she did, she looked straight into my face and asked the question I didn't want to hear.

"Mommy? Is my head hurt real bad? It sure feels funny, Mommy."

I hated to lie, but I couldn't tell this four-year-old the truth.

"Well, I think you might have cut it a little, honey. Don't worry about it; we're going to get the doctor to look at it."

With her little head starting to bob even more, yet trying to stay awake like her mother told her, Linda began to sing. The words of "Jesus Loves Me", sang in that sweet child's voice, was nearly my undoing.

My voice grew hoarse, but I sang with her. The only sound in the deathly quiet car was the two of our voices.

After the song was over, Linda did something that I will remember for the rest of my life. She looked into my eyes and in a very weary, painful voice, asked me to pray with her. I know my eyes were misty, and it felt as if a football was lodged in my throat, but I began to pray. I allowed Linda to begin. She recited the prayer that is most known to little children everywhere. It was especially poignant, given the circumstances.

"Now I lay me down to sleep
I pray the Lord my soul to keep
If I should die, before I wake
I pray the Lord, my soul to take."

MIRACLES BEYOND MEDICINE

The other adults in the car were fighting with all they had to keep from showing their grief. Me? I felt as if a huge weight had just been lifted from my shoulders.

Linda's prayer had helped me to realize that, once more, God was listening, and He was keeping my baby safe. I was still worried, but no longer terrified.

When we arrived at the hospital, there was a person standing at each door, holding it open for us to run through. We were ushered into the trauma room, the staff already waiting.

They worked on Linda's head for the next six hours. I told the doctor about Linda's cardiac history, so he gave her nothing for pain. Thankfully, she was still numb from the injury, so she felt very little. The doctor told me to stand in front of Linda's face so she could see me. He told me I would have to be Linda's anesthetic.

It was the hardest thing I've ever done in my life. I watched them cut off the ponytail I had put in just that morning. I saw them shave the scalp, then irrigate the open would. I'll admit I thought I would faint when I saw the dull white of her skull, but I didn't. Through it all, I forced myself to keep an impassive expression on my face, except when I'd smile at my daughter and tell her what a brave kid she was being.

The only time Linda cried was when they cut off her new dress. She kept asking me if I could wash it and sew it back together. I assured I could, even though I had no intention of doing so.

They put over fifty stitches in Linda's head, all without benefit of pain medication. She was a strong little girl.

As she was being wheeled to intensive care, she asked the doctor where her mother was going to sleep. The doctor told her I would in the waiting room and could see her, for a few minutes, every two hours.

Linda tried to sit up on the gurney.

"But Mommy always stays with me when I'm in the hospital. I don't think I can stay if she's not gonna be with me."

They calmed her down with soft-spoken words and gentle caresses. Nothing was said about her comments, but a nurse stopped long enough to get a lounging chair and placed it next to Linda's bed. She looked pointedly at me, then at the chair. No one actually told me I could stay with her, but their actions said I could.

Linda finally fell asleep from sheer exhaustion. I stayed awake to watch her the rest of the night. I didn't know what the morning would bring, but I was going to be there when it arrived.

The doctor walked into intensive care very early the following morning with a huge smile on his face. It couldn't be bad news, not with a smile that big!

"Mrs. Jobe? I think I have a wonderful surprise for you and this stubborn little girl. From all the tests I have conducted—all the x-rays, electrocardiogram, and blood work—the results are remarkable. It would appear that Linda has grown into her heart. Oh, the murmur is still there, but it's not as distinct as mentioned in her medical reports."

My own heart swelled to the size of the lump in my throat, but still I was afraid.

"But Doctor, what does this mean? I don't think I can fully understand what you're telling me."

"I don't doubt that, considering all you two have been through. What I'm telling you, Mrs. Jobe, is that Linda is going to be just fine. She will never have another heart attack, and she will never need surgery. I can't explain it, but that doesn't matter. My belief is, Mrs. Jobe, that we're looking at a miracle."

And a miracle it was! My baby was going to be fine; she was going to be wonderful. She would never need an operation to correct what God had already repaired.

The doctor then told me that Linda was doing so well he was going to release her to go home. He told me to watch her, make sure she didn't injure her head. I was to follow up with her regular pediatrician and have the stitches removed in two weeks. Until then, take her home and take care of her. Such easy advice, since that was all I had ever done—take care of Linda. With the joyful news of her now healthy heart, it would be a breeze.

Linda's head healed quickly. The doctor kidded her by telling her she was a hardheaded child. Linda always laughed at that. In fact, Linda laughed about almost everything after that day. And she has had reason to laugh. She can celebrate a long, happy, healthy life.

Linda is now twenty-seven years old and married. The gravely ill baby that should never have lived now has two beautiful babies of her own. Geoffrey and Zachary are just two more blessings God has given to Linda.

A Dog Named Bear

It was so quiet in the hallway, the sound of the rubber soles of my shoes bounced back at me from the brightly colored walls. Usually the artwork of the laughing clowns and the gentle animals made me smile, but not tonight.

I winced at the loud squeak the door made as I walked into Pediatric Intensive Care Unit. I made a mental note to call maintenance to oil the door hinges. Sometimes all it took was one loud noise to startle one of my patients to send their fragile hearts into cardiac arrhythmia.

The nurse in charge, Janet, smiled at me. As with most of the night shift staff, there were dark circles of fatigue smudging her eyes.

"Hello, Dr. Davis. How're things in your world? Did your wife get that promotion?"

I grinned, remembering how my wife, Carolyn, had enthusiastically hugged me when she told me she'd gotten the news she'd been promoted to Director of Nursing in the Hospice program.

"Oh yeah, she got it all right. She's floating on cloud nine and probably will be for weeks." The smile fell from my face as I glanced over the chart I had picked up.

"No change in our girl, huh?"

Janet's face reflected the frustration I was feeling. "No, no change."

"Our girl" was six-year-old Kara who had been the victim of an attempted kidnapping. She had been asleep in her bedroom when a man had cut the screen from her window and carried her from the safety of her home. He had one leg out the window when the family dog, a Chow, reached him.

"Bear" had evidently been asleep outside Kara's door, as usual, when the man entered the bedroom. The little girl had left her dollhouse blocking the door and Bear had to push it aside to get into the room. That was probably the only reason Kingston had gotten as far as he did before the dog got to him.

He sunk his teeth into the man's calf, nearly tearing the muscle from his leg. Kingston held a knife and slashed out at the dog to break his tenacious hold. During the attack, Kingston had dropped the now-screaming child onto the hard ground outside. Kara struck her head on a rock formation below the window. She was in a coma within seconds.

Kara's parents were running down the hallway, flipping lights on as they ran, which scared Kingston. He jumped to the ground and hobbled away. Neighbors later told police that amid the dog's ferocious barking, the little girl's frightened cries, they heard agonized screaming that sounded like a man's voice.

Susan and David, Kara's parents, came to an immediate halt when they got to their daughter's room. Momentarily stunned, they tried to figure out what had happened. Bear lay near the window that no longer had a protective screen, and he was barely breathing. The curtains billowed into the too-quiet room, and wet copper colored stains, which looked alarmingly like blood, covered the floor, wall, and windowsill. Their eyes darted to the bed covered with pink flowered sheets and they both gasped when they saw it empty. They jumped over Bear's unmoving body to look out the window. There they saw Kara, lying amid the rocks, deathly still. Susan screamed even as she followed David out the window, both of them smearing the blood on their pajamas.

Susan began to pick up her daughter when David put a restraining hand on her arm. He knelt beside his daughter and saw that though pale, she was still breathing.

"Don't touch her, Susan. Stay with her. I'm going to get the phone. I'll be right back."

Climbing back through the window, David glanced at the dog and surmised he was dead. He nearly fell over the dollhouse getting to the cordless phone in the living room.

Within minutes, sirens could be heard winding through the residential streets of the housing development. The paramedics had jumped from the ambulance as it was still rocking on its chassis. They rushed to the place where a distraught young mother knelt in the grass, her sobbing loud in the night. Lights began coming on in the surrounding houses.

Kara's breathing was becoming increasingly labored. During the rapid assessment done by the ambulance crew, a small depression was found in Kara's skull. As she was still breathing on her own, an oxygen mask was placed over her face for transport. A cervical collar was put in place to guard against spinal injury and an IV was started.

As they worked, police officers fired questions at the two adults looming over the medical crew. When they determined the parents knew little more than the officers did, they stepped aside so Kara could be placed on a waiting gurney and moved quickly toward the ambulance. Susan followed her little girl into the back of the vehicle as the crew told David which hospital they were taking his child to.

The siren recommenced its plaintive wail as David pushed through police to grab his car keys. He then realized he was locked out of the house and would have to climb back through the window. When he had both feet inside the room, he heard Bear whimper. In spite of the confusion of all that was happening, David had the presence of mind to be shocked that the dog was still alive. He turned toward the window to see an officer standing there, watching him. He asked if someone could take the dog to get medical attention, his voice husky with unshed tears.

I was getting as much information from Susan as I could when David ran into the emergency room. His hair was as wild as his eyes and his bloody pajama shirt flapped as he ran toward us.

"Where is she? How's Kara? Is she okay? What happened?"

Neither his wife nor I could give him most of those answers. I escorted them both to an empty waiting room to speak with them.

"I've only had time to do a very fast, very brief assessment of Kara at the moment. I wanted to find out as much as I could before I went back in there. All I can tell you now is that she's unconscious. There's been severe injury to the occipital part of her skull; that's at the back of her head. I can't really give you more information until we get x-rays and probably a CAT scan done. Can you tell me what happened?

Susan's voice was shaky and her trembling hands fluttered as she spoke. "All we know is that we heard Bear, that's our dog, barking. We ran into Kara's room and she wasn't there…" She squeezed her eyes tightly at the image in her mind. David continued.

"Bear was on the floor. I thought he was dead… There was blood everywhere! The screen had been cut off the window. Kara was outside, lying on the ground… Susan stayed with her while I called an ambulance. The cops came and…" He seemed too distraught to pull his thoughts together. I believed I had a rough idea of what had happened, though.

I took their hands and held them as I looked into their faces. "I promise you that we'll do everything we can to help Kara. I'm going to go order the tests now. We'll do them as quickly as we can and then I'll come back out and tell you what we've found. I know this has to be very hard on both of you, and I wish there was some way to make it easier. Is there anyone you want us to contact for you? I can have the hospital chaplain come down, if you want him. Or you can have the nurse call someone for you."

They both numbly shook their heads, clinging to each other's hands as they stared at the floor.

It wasn't very long after my conversation with Kara's parents that I was looking at the x-rays and reading the radiologist's report. Even though I had ordered a CAT scan, what I saw on the black and gray film was glaringly obvious. I was certain further testing would only corroborate what I already knew. Without surgery, Kara's condition would only worsen.

I hurried down the hall to watch the computer monitor illustrate the degree of injury as the big machine scanned the girl's brain. The test was just coming to an end when I walked back into the waiting room. David and Susan both stood as I came into the room, their pale faces hopeful as they looked into my eyes. I only wished I could give them better news than they were going to receive.

"Let's sit down." They glanced at each other, their faces blanching even more as they sensed bad news.

"There is a compound fracture of the skull. This means the bone is depressed and driven inward. The only way to correct this is a craniotomy, or surgery of the skull."

Susan buried her face in her husband's shoulder to stifle the sobs. David hitched a deep breath, his eyes bloodshot from trying to hold back his own tears. He had to clear his throat before he could ask the dreaded questions.

"Is there brain damage? Is she going to die? Just how bad is it, Doc?"

"David, I can't really answer that truthfully until after surgery. I can tell you now that Kara is still breathing on her own, and that's a good sign. Anytime we have a head injury that doesn't have to go on a ventilator, we're optimistic. But, unless we get her to surgery soon, the brain may start to swell, and then we'll run into even worse problems. I can't tell you what to do, I can only advise you to sign the papers for an operation as soon as possible."

Susan spoke, though it was difficult to understand what she was saying for the tears in her speech. "Will she make it through an operation?"

At times like this, I almost wished the medical field was as it used to be in terms of telling family members little of the truth. Almost.

"I can't answer that, either. I can tell you it looks good, but I can't give you any guarantees. She's young, she's strong, and we got her here early after the accident…"

David's face turned crimson with suppressed anger. "It wasn't an accident! Someone did this to her. And if I ever find out who did it…"

Since I had a daughter of my own, very close to Kara's age, I could empathize with his anger. But I wanted to pull him back to the reality of what we were facing.

"Do you agree to surgery? I don't mean to sound crass, but we really need to get a move on this immediately."

David's eyes focused and Susan lifted her head to nod. He sighed deeply. "Yeah, have someone give us the papers to sign."

"I'll have the nurse get them in here. I'm so sorry this has happened. I can't say I know how you feel, because none of us do unless we've been through something like this. I've got to go for now, but I'll be back as soon as I can. I've got a little girl I've got to make well again." I tried to smile as I shook their hands.

The operation took longer than the parents' patience lasted. By the time I got back to them, David and Susan had reached the end of their rope. They met me at the door of the waiting room and I felt as if they were holding their breath, fearing the worst.

"Well, the surgery is over. Kara is in PICU. She's on a ventilator…"

I stopped when Susan gasped and grabbed her husband's arm. It was at that moment that my own words came back to me. I'd told them it was a good sign Kara hadn't gone on a ventilator when she first got to us.

"Okay, wait a minute. Calm down. Kara being on a ventilator after surgery is a common practice. This doesn't mean she's worse. It merely means she's gone through a very rough ordeal and needs help to breathe for now. We'll wean her off, a little at a time."

I could see their shoulders relax, just a little. Susan then asked for more details.

"We've relieved the pressure that the fracture was putting on the brain. She's getting medication in her IV to keep down swelling, too. There is reaction to pain stimulus, and movement of all her extremities. These are all good signs."

David asked, "Okay, so when can we see her?"

"Right now, if you want to. I want you to be prepared for seeing a lot of machines and tubes attached to her. Her head is wrapped in bandages and she's very pale. There's a tube in her mouth that leads to the ventilator…"

They stepped around me, interrupting me to ask where PICU was located. I didn't blame them. If I had been in their shoes, I would've left the doctor still talking and rush off to see my child, too.

"It's on the seventh floor. Get off the elevators and turn right."

Dawn was peeking over the skyline when I climbed into my car. Glancing in the rearview mirror, I saw the familiar dark smears beneath my eyes. I felt older than my years.

It seemed only minutes had passed since I'd left when I walked back into PICU. I carried the chart with me to Kara's bed. As I pulled my stethoscope from my pocket, Janet continued to talk.

"Pulmonary has been unable to decrease the oxygen level on the ventilator. Weaning parameters aren't good. And even though we're still getting movement of the extremities, she's not waking up."

I met David entering the unit as I was leaving.

"Hi, Doc. What's going on with Kara? Why isn't she waking up? Can't we do something else?"

"David, sometimes this takes longer than others. Tests indicate there is no brain swelling but Kara's coma is deep. She should wake up at any given minute. Why she hasn't, we can't tell you. When you're with her, talk to her. Talk about things at home, things she likes to do, any pets she has... Hey, how did it turn out with the dog?"

It was the first small smile I'd seen David wear. "Bear is one tough canine. The man stabbed him between the ribs and there was a lot of internal bleeding that the vet said should've killed him. They operated on him last night and he's already trying to walk around this morning."

"That's good to hear, and Kara would like to hear it, too. Tell her all about Bear. Tell her funny stories about him, about anything. Reach in there and pull her out of that coma."

David nodded and walked to his daughter. I punched the button for the elevator with more force than was necessary. I headed for ER to wait on the next trauma.

Fifteen minutes later I had my first patient. I usually treat pediatric patients, but we were short-handed. The nurse asked me to look at an adult male that had just arrived. Even though he was in a great deal of pain, he'd driven himself to the hospital. He lay on the examination table, writhing in agony.

"Mr., uh…" I glanced down at the chart. "Mr. Kingston, what's going on? You have a problem with your leg, according to your chart. Can you tell me what happened?"

He practically snarled his reply. "Yeah, a damned dog is what happened. Stupid dog tried to take my leg off."

"Oh? When did this happen? The wound isn't fresh." I gingerly touched the bruised flesh around the jagged tear, causing the patient to nearly jump from the table. It was a nasty looking injury, and I knew it hurt when I touched it, but I had no choice.

"Last night. It happened last night. I was walking home from the store when this big ugly dog came out of nowhere and tried to rip my leg off. I thought he was going to kill me. I probably should've gone to my family doctor but I kept thinking my leg would get better, until it started gettin' all puffy. I thought about infection when it started throbbing this evening."

Trying to take his mind off the pain as much as possible, I kept asking questions. "Man, I bet that was scary. Big dog coming at you in the dark. Do you know if the dog has had his shots? How'd you get him to let you go?"

"I had my knife with me and stuck it in him. I got him in the side and the mangy mutt fell over dead. That'll be the last time he ever bites someone."

There was something more alarming here than the fact this man had killed a dog. A detail that I was missing kept skating around my head as I worked to clean the wound, but I just couldn't grasp it. I hate to say that the man had to almost give me the answer, himself, before it finally occurred to me. "Bear. What a stupid name for a dog…"

"What did you say?"

"Bear—that's the dog's name."

"Oh, uh huh. What time did this happen last night?"

Suspicion crept into his face. "About midnight, I guess. Why do you ask? What difference does the time make?"

"I need to know about how long you've had this infection simmering in this leg. I'm going to have to clean it deeper. This is a bad bite. Hold on, I'll be right back. I don't have all the supplies I need in here."

He sat up on the table as if he were going to leave. To push his distrust aside, I motioned a nurse into the room.

"Linda, will you give Sam an injection of Valium and Versed? I'm going to have to do a debridement of the wound and I want him to be relaxed." I turned back to the patient. "Sam, this injection will help with the pain, and after I'm done, you won't even remember the procedure. That's the great thing about this shot."

Sam grinned. "Sure, whatever you say. You're the doctor." He lay back down on the examination table, already turning on his side for the needle.

"Be right back, Sam."

I closed the door behind me and quickly stepped to the nurse's station.

"Denyse, will you call the police?" Denyse's eyes opened wide in question.

"Tell them I think the man that tried to kidnap Kara is here, with a bad dog bite." She picked up the phone before I finished the sentence.

I cleaned and dressed Sam Kingston's leg wound and he didn't flinch. After the effects of the drugs had subsided, the police were there to question him. It didn't take them long to get a confession. Kingston had a long rap sheet, but this was the first time he'd ever attempted kidnapping. He told police that he figured he could get money from the girl's parents if he took her. His previous crimes had been stealing cars and money. Where he was going, he didn't have to worry about a car or money to buy gas for it.

It took almost another twenty-four hours for Kara to fully awaken. It was soon apparent there was no lasting damage done to her brain. Then, with the incredible resilience of children, she seemed to recover overnight.

I asked to be the one that rolled Kara's wheelchair to the entrance of the hospital on her release. David stood beside the car and Susan jumped out to kiss her little girl. Through the open door came a huge ball of black fur, leaping toward Kara.

"Bear!" Kara was giggling and her beloved pet stood on his back legs to cover her face in kisses. Even as she wiped the wet spots, she nuzzled the dog's neck with her face.

"Oh Bear, I've missed you. Have you been a good boy? Good ol' Bear. Dr. Davis, you like my dog?"

I leaned over to pet the gentle canine that had been vicious enough to save this child's life.

"Yeah Kara, I think he's great. Bear. What a great name for a dog."

Last Chance

"Yes Mom, we'll be gone for just two days. Oh, I don't know why Nick thinks this is gonna help, but he harped about it for weeks. You sure you don't mind watching the kids while we're gone?"

I listened while my mother complained this was nothing but a waste of time and money.

"I know, I know, but I'm tired of arguing about it. If going away for the weekend is what Nick wants to prove to himself that this marriage is over, then that's what he'll get. I just want to get it over with so he'll sign the divorce papers. It'll be so much easier if he'll agree to an uncontested divorce."

I hadn't heard the kitchen door open behind me and didn't know he was standing there, listening, until he dropped his lunch box onto the kitchen counter. I turned to see him staring at me with a mixture of anger and something close to hatred on his still-handsome face that used to cause my heart to skip a beat. His hands clinched into fists were held rigidly at his sides, hands that used to caress me with such a gentle and loving touch it sent a chill down my spine. But that was all in the past.

"Mom, I've got to go."

She began to protest, wanting to tell me again, in unrelenting detail, what a loser my husband was, at least in her humble opinion.

"Mom, Nick is home and I've got to go."

I hung up as she was launching into another tirade about the man I had married. I turned to look at him, waiting on him to dig into me. I didn't have long to wait.

"Rhonda, I can see that you're giving this your best shot. I'm sure I don't deserve your kindness, your loving understanding. Thank you, sweetheart, for giving our marriage one more try, knowing what a worthless piece of garbage I've proven to be."

I knew my face was twisted into a grimace of annoyance, but I didn't care. I hadn't cared for a long time now.

"This is your idea, Nick, not mine. Don't think that just because you're making some last-ditch effort that it's going to work. I, myself, think it's too little, too late. So unless you have some sort of magical solution, this 'weekend alone, just the two of us' is an exercise in futility. Just remember your promise. If I agreed to go away this weekend, you agreed to sign the papers next week."

"What I agreed to was if you sincerely made an effort to save this relationship, and if it still didn't work out, I'd talk to your divorce attorney next week. But if you're not even going to make an honest effort..."

"What is your definition of an honest effort, Nick? If that means that I'm going to fawn all over you, that I'm going to welcome you back into my bed, that I'm going to forgive and forget all the lies, the hurtful words..."

I saw the muscles of his jaw tighten in an anger that was the foundation of our marriage lately.

"What it means, Rhonda, is that we talk, and that we listen. That means we really, really listen. It means that we leave the anger and petty fights here in this house. It means that we try to figure out what went wrong and if there's anything left to salvage. It means that staying together for the kids isn't enough. It means we have to decide if there's any reason to keep on trying."

I could feel my own temper flaring, reaching the point of no return.

"Hey baby, I can save you a few bucks and a lot of time. Let me answer all your questions right now, this very minute. No, going away for some sort of healing weekend isn't going to save us. No amount of talking, or rather screaming, is going to change the facts. I'm tired of you rarely being home, and when you are, if you're even awake, you're yelling at me. I can't do enough to make you happy, to satisfy the Neanderthal in you. My job is just as demanding, just as stressful, as your job. I'm as tired as you are, yet I still have my 'other job' to do when I get home. Just once I'd like to see you wash a dish, cook a meal, throw a load of clothes into the washer."

"Rhonda, is that what this is all about—the fact that I don't wash a load of clothes? All you had to do was ask. I don't mind helping out, but you come home and hit the ground running. I'd like to see you relax more, just sit down and maybe watch the news with me."

"Oh God, of course I hit the ground running when I get home after work. If I don't do it, it won't get done. Just ask you for help? Did it ever, just once, occur to you to help me without my having to ask you? Anyway, it doesn't matter. I've seen the way you do the laundry the few times you've done it. No thanks, it's easier to just do it myself. But this isn't just about washing clothes and you damned well know it." He chose to ignore that last remark, I noted.

"You don't have any intention of trying to work this out, do you, Rhonda? You don't even…"

"Oh for the love of God, will you just start putting the things in the car and let's get going? We have to be there by six o'clock to make the room reservation."

His deep sigh caused my own jaw muscles to tense.

"Just let me take a quick shower and I'll pack my suitcase."

"Never mind packing, Nick. Like everything else, I've done it myself."

He stalked out of the room and I soon heard water running in the shower.

He's not so stupid that he truly believes all this is over his not helping with housework. He knows the reason, and her name is Debbie.

The two-hour drive to the motel was a quiet one. For all of his protestations of wanting to communicate by talking—really talking, and listening—really listening, Nick was a stone statue behind the steering wheel.

I sat in the car as Nick went to the motel office to get the room key. A small part of me ached at the sight of him walking back to the car with his head low. I angrily pushed the feeling away.

The heavy silence continued as we emptied the car of the things we'd need for the weekend away from home.

Weekend away from home. That sounds more like pleasure instead of this shrieking, grating sound of running your fingernails across a chalkboard. Nick should've saved what he's spending on this forty-eight hour fiasco and used it for his attorney fees.

"Rhonda, would you grab my laptop computer for me? My hands are full."

"Why of course, your majesty. Anything else I can do for you, my lord?"

"Yeah, you can lose the sarcasm, babe. I don't know why I'm doing this…"

I snorted, knowing the sound angered him. I was rewarded with the predictable response.

"Will you, please, stop making that irritating sound? No words could better express how much you hate me."

"Hate you? Sorry to disappoint you yet again, Nickie. I don't care enough to waste that much emotion. That takes more energy than I'm willing to expend on this marriage."

He reached behind the driver's seat and savagely jerked the laptop from the car.

"Careful, Nickiepoo. You don't want to lose your temper, do you?"

He glared at me. "If I hadn't been careful I would've lost my temper with you months ago, Snoogums."

I shrugged. "Oh well, maybe you should've thought about all that before you had an affair."

Nick, blushing, glanced around the parking lot, no doubt looking for anyone that may have overheard what I'd just said. "You think we could at least get inside the room before you start this again?"

I pulled a look of surprise over my face. "Oh, I'm sorry. Did I embarrass you? Well ya know what? I was embarrassed plenty of times when everyone, except me, knew you were fooling around.

Wow, was my face red!"

Nick bit his lip against the comment he started to make, then walked over and unlocked the door to room seven. I heard him laugh without humor as he joked about the number seven not being so lucky after all.

"Yeah Nick, just like the seven years we've been married—very lucky for both of us, huh?"

"Give it a rest okay, Rhonda?"

"Oh yeah, I'm gonna give it a long, long rest, Nickie."

"You know I hate it when you call me that."

"Yeah, I know."

His lips were a pencil-thin line in his face but it didn't bother me. I'd seen that expression in my own mirror for several months now—since the name Debbie slithered into our lives.

Nick dropped the bags on the floor, then turned to me. "Where do you want to go for dinner?"

I shrugged. "It doesn't matter much to me."

"Nothing matters much to you anymore, does it, Ro?"

He knew I hated it when he called me that name. I let it go, figuring turn-about's fair play.

"No, not much matters to me lately. The kids, my job..."

"But not us, right? When did you fall out of love with me, Rhonda?"

I could feel my face burning from the anger I was barely able to contain. "Oh, right about the time you decided to cheat on me, I guess."

"You fell out of love long before you decided to start accusing me of cheating on you."

"It's not just an accusation, Nick, so don't try to pull that..."

His raised voice could still rattle me, though I tried to not let it show. "I never, ever, not once, had sex with another woman."

"You're so full of..."

"C'mon Rhonda, let's get this out in the open. After all, that's why we came here this weekend, isn't it?"

"No, that's why you came here. Me, I only came to pacify you so you'd finally get it through your head that this marriage is over."

"Okay, if that's the only reason, why don't you just humor me then.

Tell me all the evidence you have against me. Tell me how you're so sure I cheated on you."

"Oh, for God's sake, you know exactly what I have on you, Nick." His smile was sardonic. "Remember? Humor me, please. Let's pretend I haven't heard all of it before and tell me what you know. Not what you imagine, but what you know."

"Alright Nick, let's start with square one, shall we?"

He settled onto the end of the king-sized bed as if awaiting the rerun of a pleasurable performance. "Please, go on."

"The first thing was finding her phone number."

Nick held up his hand. "Just a small side note here. You found it while sneaking through my pants pocket."

"I wouldn't have been doing that if I hadn't felt there was something wrong, now would I?"

He nodded his head in agreement.

"On the piece of paper with her phone number was that stupid note: 'Call me anytime, Nickie'."

"And so you just assumed that since I had her number that I called her."

"Why the hell else would you keep it if you didn't intend to call her?"

His face blushed. "It could've been because I was amazed that any woman was interested in me. I mean, you'd pretty much shut me out of your life after you had Jeremy."

"Oh, don't try to lay this on me, Nick! Having Jeremy was hard. I was afraid of getting pregnant again."

"I understood that. That's why I had the vasectomy, so you wouldn't have to be scared anymore."

"Did you have it for me, or for yourself?"

"For myself?"

"Well, it'd be one way of fooling around and not getting caught."

"Oh, good grief, Rhonda! Do you know how silly that sounds?"

I ignored him. "Then there was the time you were actually seen with her."

"Seen in a public restaurant, right? Surely if I were cheating on you

I'd have been more discreet, taken her to someplace in another town where no one knew me."

I smiled. "You might have thought it was very clever of you to do it right under my nose, Nick. I'll bet you were laughing about it while you made love."

Brushing that comment aside, "So your friends saw me there, raced home to call you, saying they saw things that never happened."

I shook my head in anger. "They only told me the truth. And if you weren't having an affair, why were you with her?"

"I admit I took her to dinner. Hell, I'll even admit I was flattered. It was tempting, and it certainly crossed my mind to do it. But I didn't, Rhonda. I was so lonely, needed the attention, the desire of a woman, but I didn't want just any woman. I wanted you, but you didn't want me. How long had it been by that time, Rhonda? Tell me how long it'd been since you had let me touch you."

I couldn't stop myself from screaming at him. "I don't give a damn! There is no reason to cheat on your wife. I loved you, Nick! God help me, I had loved you so much."

"You always say that in the past tense. Don't you love me anymore, Rhonda?"

"No, I don't. I haven't loved you since you went to bed with another woman."

"I swear to you I never did more than have dinner with her. God knows I didn't. But you'll never believe that, will you? But it's the truth, just like the fact that I still love you, very much, and I always will."

"Oh, save it, will you, Nick? I'm so tired of the fighting, and the lies."

"I've never lied to you, Rhonda. I took an attractive woman to dinner, talked about something other than bills and dirty diapers. That's it, one dinner, and I was tried and convicted without just cause. I love you too much to ever do anything more. I'd never want to lose you, and I'd do anything to keep us together."

"It's too late. Why can't I make you see that?"

His chin rested on his chest for a moment. When he raised his eyes, I could see the tears shining in them. "I guess I finally see it,

Rhonda. I finally get it. No matter that I didn't really do anything wrong, no matter that I'd do anything to have you love me again, it's over."

"I could never trust you again. I did once, and look what happened."

I was sure people in the parking lot heard his anguished cry. "Nothing! I did nothing, Rhonda!"

I would have died before I would have admitted that a tiny seed of doubt had been planted. Oh, what if he was telling the truth? What if he had truly never cheated on me? No, I couldn't let myself be swayed by pity at his tears—his phony tears. I remained stone-faced.

He wiped his tears with his shirtsleeve. "This is useless. I'd hoped that we could save it, save us, but it's not going to happen. We might as well go back home."

"I think that's a good idea."

His deep sigh was full of pain. "Okay, I'll take the room key back to the office and we can head back home. You can file for the divorce next Monday. I won't fight you anymore."

He walked slowly to the door, then turned back to look at me. "I still love you, Rhonda. I meant that as much as the first time I said it."

He opened the door and stepped into the sunshine. "No, I mean it more now that I ever have." He pulled the door behind him; the lock caught on the edge of the door. I took a step to close the door, then shrugged, and turned to the bathroom to run a comb through my hair. I stared at the woman that looked back at me, thought how much older she was looking, then made a face at her.

The door opened and I began to walk into the other room to grab a suitcase to carry to the car. It wasn't Nick that walked into the room.

Two men that I'd never seen before pushed the door closed. The smile on their faces chilled me.

"Who are you? What do you want?"

The burly man with long dark hair chuckled. "Well lady, we heard all the commotion and just thought we'd check to make sure you're okay in here."

I was rooted to the spot, my mouth almost too dry to form words.

"Yes, I'm okay. Just a little family squabble, you know how that goes. Nick, that's my husband, will be back any second. Yeah, just a small argument, that's all. Thanks for your concern, but we're fine."

The smaller man, lanky blonde hair thinning on top, displayed yellowed teeth when he grinned. "Well, we'll just stick around and wait on Nick. You know, just to make sure everything's really okay."

"Oh, that's not necessary, really it isn't. You can go on. We're getting ready to go back home as soon as Nick gets back from the front office."

The bigger man looked at the smaller man and smiled. The smile wasn't a nice one. "What d'ya think, Sam? You think we oughta just mosey on out of here, leave the lil lady alone to wait on ol' Nick?"

"Oh no, Jim, I don't think that is such a good idea. No, not a good idea at all."

My knees were shaking and it felt as if my head would explode. "Honestly, it's nothing. I'll be perfectly fine waiting here alone."

"Perfectly fine, eh?"

I nodded my head vigorously. Both men shook their heads in denial. I was about to break into tears when the door opened again. My heart skipped a beat when I saw Nick hesitate after he stepped into the room. He looked at me, a questioning look on his face.

"Rhonda?"

Before I could speak, Jim kicked the door shut. "Join the party, Nickie."

Instant anger crossed Nick's face when he began to assimilate the situation. "Who the hell are you? What do you want with us?"

Sam walked over and put his arm around my shoulders. "We heard all the feudin' and fussin'. We thought we'd just come in and see what's going on."

I tried to pull free, but he only tightened his hold on me.

Nick started to lunge for Sam. "Get your damned hands off her!"

Jim slammed his fist into Nick's stomach, knocking the air from his lungs. "You need to just chill out there, Nickie."

I again tried to break free of Sam's hold to get to Nick. I didn't see the blow coming. Before I knew it, I was lying on the floor, face down.

I pushed myself up and put my hand to my face. I moaned when I touched my nose and felt the warm stickiness of blood. I was still lying there when I felt rough hands pulling me to my feet.

Nick bellowed with animal rage when he saw my face. Before he could move Jim had pulled out a gun and slammed it into the side of Nick's head. Nick hit the floor with a hard thud.

I screamed and scrabbled across the room on my hands and knees. "Nick, oh Nick!" A kick in the side of my ribs knocked me backward.

"Shut up, bitch. If you scream one more time I'm gonna kill Nickie here while you watch. You got that, Ro?"

Clutching my side, all I could do was nod my head. When I could breathe I scooted over to Nick. The two men watched me almost disinterestedly. They stood side by side, whispering. I was more interested in Nick than what these two filthy animals may be planning at the moment.

I cradled his head in my lap. "Nick? Honey? Honey, please speak to me. Please, Nick."

He opened his eyes and I could tell that one was beginning to blacken and swell shut. "Shh, Rhonda. I'm okay, baby, I'm okay."

Outside the room I heard a loud noise and it took me a few seconds to recognize what it was. Someone was using a bullhorn to speak to the two men that were holding us hostage. The booming voice sounded as hollow as my own hope for escape.

"Sam, Jim, listen to me. This is the police. There's no use in fighting us, boys. Just come out with your hands raised in the air."

I looked at the two men to gage their reaction.

"Yeah Rhonda, it's really the cops. See, we just made a small withdrawal at the bank across the street a few minutes ago. Unfortunately for you our driver chickened out. Imagine how ticked off we were when we ran out of the bank to find our car gone. We were running across the street when we heard all the yellin', so we just dashed in here."

I could hear the tremor in my voice when I spoke. "Let us go, please just let us go. We've got two kids."

Sam's voice was mocking, "'Please let us go home.' Lady, I don't give a damn if you've got twenty kids, you're my ticket out of here. You're not going anywhere until I say so."

Jim chuckled, "Yeah, and we might just have us a party, Rhonda-girl. What d'ya say? How's 'bout we leave ol' Nickie here tied up and go for a long ride? 'Course we gotta get rid of those cops outside, first."

The bullhorn outside blared back into the room. "Boys, just let the Carsons go. They're not part of this. They're innocent bystanders."

Sam smirked. "That's not the way I understand it, right Nickie?"

Jim said, "Yeah, we heard you was two-steppin' on the wrong dance floor, Nickie. So I'm sure you'll understand when we dance a time or two with your lady here."

Nick lunged for the two smirking outlaws; hands already doubled into fists. The gunshot that knocked him back to the floor was loud in the small room. He lay on his back, not moving.

"No! Oh God no!" I was rushing across the room to my husband when I heard the second shot and felt the immediate burning pain in my leg. I crumpled to the floor next to Nick.

Sam yelled, "Jim, why'd you do that? Why'd you shoot her?"

"I knew she was gonna be a problem, just knew it. We told her to shut up."

Sam backhanded his partner, but before Jim could retaliate, the front door crashed open. The room was filled with uniforms and drawn guns. Sam and Jim fell to the floor under the weight of several police officers.

I held Nick's still body, his pale face pressed against my chest. I rocked him back and forth much the same way I rocked our children. I stroked his head as I watched the large blood stain spread wider across the left side of his shirt.

I yelled into the swirling commotion around me, "Would someone please help him?" Louder then, "Someone help my husband!"

Nick, whispering, trying to say something, caught my attention. "No baby, it's going to be alright. We'll get you to a hospital, Nick. You're going to be fine, you'll see. Shh, don't try to talk, honey."

He was struggling so hard to tell me something. I leaned close to his mouth. "I didn't do it, Rhonda. I swear I never cheated on you." He pressed his lips to my cheek. "I love you, Rhonda." Then no more words. His eyes closed and his body relaxed against mine.

I cried and began to scream. Gentle hands pulled Nick from me and lay him onto a gurney. They ran with him toward an ambulance that was waiting with lights flashing across the darkness of rapidly approaching night. I was numb, my mind refusing to focus on the fact that Nick was probably dead.

After a paramedic checked me out I discovered the bullet had only grazed my leg. It had already stopped bleeding. An officer escorted me from the room to a patrol car. We raced to the hospital, fighting against traffic and death.

They took me to a private waiting room at the hospital. A nurse handed me a cup of coffee that I just held in my hand, not drinking, until someone else took it from me. A doctor sat beside me and I stiffened.

"Mrs. Carson, your husband is in surgery."

Hope burned bright, illuminating the dingy gray walls around me. "Nick's alive? Oh my God, I thought..."

"Mrs. Carson, Rhonda, listen to me."

His words sent chills down my spine. I threw my hands over my ears, not wanting to hear what he had to say next. He pulled my arms down and looked into my eyes, forcing me to hear his words.

"I can't promise you that he's going to live, Rhonda. There is massive damage and he's lost a lot of blood. We got to him quickly, but still, in cases like this..."

I grabbed his hand. "What do you mean, in cases like this?"

The doctor's face was compassionate, yet sad. "Even if he makes it through the operation, with a large loss of blood there could be a chance of brain damage."

I felt myself begin to rock back and forth again, just as I had when I held Nick's body in the motel room. "Nooo, not Nick, not Nick."

"Rhonda, please stay with me. I need you to be strong. Nick's going to need you to be strong." He motioned for a nurse to sit beside me. "Rhonda, I'm going to go back upstairs. I'll send down word of our progress as soon as I can."

The nurse took my hand. "Rhonda, is there anyone I can call for you? Any family that you want here with you?"

My eyes flooded with tears as I thought of our kids waiting at home for Mommy and Daddy. I began to see our lives from a child's point of view. Their lives had consisted of either cold silence or hot arguments for so months, too many months. And it had been for nothing. I had been wrong all this time. Nick hadn't had an affair. His worst crime had been to have dinner with a woman that made him feel attractive, wanted. He had dinner with a woman that was making him feel the way I should have made him feel.

Oh God, please. Give me another chance. Don't let my own stupidity take Nick's life.

The night was growing into morning when I felt a familiar presence walk into the room. I looked up into the sorrowful eyes of my mother. I ran across the room to be held in her supportive, loving embrace.

"Have you heard any news, Rhonda?"

"The last thing I heard was about an hour ago. It's still too close to call, Mom. We still don't know if he's going to make it."

She walked me back to the lounge, holding my cold hand in hers. "Rhonda, no matter what, we'll get through this. You're going to be fine. I'm here to help you through this, honey."

"I know that, Mom, and it means a lot to me. But I want Nick. I just want Nick to be okay."

"Well honey, if he had only…"

"Don't say it, Mom, just don't say it. I made a mistake."

"No dear, you didn't make a mistake. Nick made a mistake…"

"I'm telling you, Mom, Nick didn't do anything. I was wrong— wrong in so many ways."

Her face was sad, yet angry. "How can you say that, Rhonda? You worked, took care of the kids…"

"Yeah Mom, I did. And that's all I did. I forgot, somewhere along the way, that I was Nick's wife before I was ever the mother of our kids. I held my children to me, letting him go when I did."

"I don't believe this! You're honestly blaming yourself for his affair!"

"He never had an affair, Mom."

"What? We all know…"

"We don't know anything, Mom. He had dinner with a woman and our imaginations turned it into an affair. He didn't sleep with her, Mom. Dinner, that's all it was, just dinner."

"And you believe that, don't you, Rhonda? I'm sorry Nick got hurt, but the facts remain the same."

"The fact is, Nick was treated unfairly. Oh, he's not totally blameless, he did his share of arguing, too, but I was the one that destroyed our marriage. And if God will give me a second chance, I'm going to make the most of it."

As if in answer to my plea, the surgeon walked into the room. His expression seemed to be guarded, so I couldn't prepare myself before he delivered the news about Nick.

"Rhonda, I'm Doctor Sims. I wanted to give you an update of Nick's condition. He's now out of surgery and in intensive care. I think that all things considered, it went very well. The damage to the heart wasn't quite as extensive as we had first thought, so we were able to repair it completely."

"You said 'all things considered'. What did you mean by that?"

"Well, there is still the problem of Nick losing so much of his blood volume. Since he was still in a coma when we wheeled him into surgery, we had no way to determine if there was compromise to brain function. And even if he had been conscious, brain activity could have been impaired and we couldn't tell until he wakes up from surgery."

"So he's going to be all right, physically. But mentally?"

"We'll have to wait and see, Rhonda. I want you to know he may not come through this as you hope. He may never again be the man you knew before today. Let's just hope for the best."

I took a deep, quivering breath. "Can I see him now?"

"Yes, but please, just for a few moments. He's still unconscious and we'd rather allow him to awaken at his own pace. Later today we'll discuss longer visits, okay? Let's take this one step at a time, Rhonda."

I stood up and shook his hand. He smiled and patted my back. I'm sure he meant for that smile to be comforting. It was anything but that. I knew without his saying a word that this doctor believed the man I'd married was gone.

The cloying smell that's exclusive to hospitals assaulted my swollen nose when I walked into intensive care. I felt my breath catch in my chest when I saw Nick lying there with wires leading to different machines.

His face was the same shade of white as the sheets he lay on. His chest rose and fell in rhythm with the ventilator that breathed for him. I lifted his limp hand from the bed and kissed it. I saw the blood beneath the nails that the staff hadn't had time to clean before he was taken to the operating room.

"I'm so sorry, Nick. Get well, honey, and let's go home to start our lives all over again. Together we can make it right again, better than ever before. But you've got to prove them all wrong. You've got to wake up and let them see you're still you. I love you, Nick. Please come back to us."

Twenty-four hours doesn't seem like a long time, but it's enough time to change history. That's how long it took for Nick to come out of the deep coma he was in. The doctors were worried, and I'd heard it whispered that they feared Nick didn't want to wake up. They said he was hiding in his coma. I prayed they were wrong.

God, let Nick know that things are different, that I'm different. Please tell him to wake up, to come home to me. Tell him that I love him.

I was standing there when Nick woke up. He tried to smile, then feeling the tube between his lips, he reached up to pull it out. I grabbed his arm, pulling it down to the bed.

"You can't do that, honey. Now that you're waking up, when you start breathing on your own, they'll pull that tube out."

His eyes asked questions his lips couldn't.

"You're going to be fine, Nick. You sure gave all of us a scare, but you've come through surgery in great shape. Your heart is going to be good as new. The biggest problem you're going to have is working out the soreness." I smiled as he lay there quietly, staring into my eyes, still questioning.

"And we're going to be fine, too, Nick. I'm so sorry for doubting you, for not believing you. We've been given another chance, honey. All you have to do is get well, we can work on the rest when we get home."

He lifted my hand to lay it against his cheek, his eyes never leaving my face. He closed his eyes in sleep, and a solitary tear dropped onto the pillow.

Ten days later Nick was released from the hospital. I'd rented a van, removed the back seats, and put in a temporary bed. We were on our way home, and the kids were waiting.

I'd picked up a few things at a grocery store before I picked him up at the hospital entrance. I'd pulled the curtains closed on all the windows so Nick could sleep. We'd driven for about an hour when I pulled off into a shaded area at the side of the road. Nick had been dozing on the bed in the back. I tried to be quiet removing the food for our picnic. I was reaching for napkins that had fallen out of the paper bag. Nick woke and grabbed my arm, grinning. I recognized that look, even though I hadn't seen it for a long, long time.

I laughed. "I thought the doctors said there was no brain damage. You've got to be crazy, Nick. It's only been a few days since you had surgery..."

The low growl in his throat was filled with desire. I allowed myself to be pulled down beside him on the bed. As Nick's lips covered my own, I thought, "Doctors didn't know everything, did they?"

...and the miracles continue.

Printed in the United States
16779LVS00001B/181